ACCLAIM FOR COLLEEN COBLE

"Coble's atmospheric and suspenseful series launch should appeal to fans of Tracie Peterson and other authors of Christian romantic suspense."

—*Library Journal* review of *Tidewater Inn*

"Romantically tense, but with just the right touch of danger, this cowboy love story is surprisingly clever—and pleasingly sweet."

—USAToday.com
review of *Blue Moon Promise*

"Colleen Coble will keep you glued to each page as she shows you the beauty of God's most primitive land and the dangers it hides."

—www.RomanceJunkies.com

"[An] outstanding, completely engaging tale that will have you on the edge of your seat . . . A must-have for all fans of romantic suspense!"

—TheRomanceReadersConnection.
com review of *Anathema*

"Colleen Coble lays an intricate trail in *Without a Trace* and draws the reader on like a hound with a scent."

—*Romantic Times*, 4½ stars

"Coble's historical series just keeps getting better with each entry."

—*Library Journal* starred review
of *The Lightkeeper's Ball*

"Don't ever mistake [Coble's] for the fluffy romances with a little bit of suspense. She writes solid suspense, and she ties it all together beautifully with a wonderful message."

—LifeinReviewBlog.com review of *Lonestar Angel*

"This book has everything I enjoy: mystery, romance, and suspense. The characters are likable, understandable, and I can relate to them."

—TheFriendlyBookNook.com

"[M]ystery, danger, and intrigue as well as romance, love, and subtle inspiration. *The Lightkeeper's Daughter* is a 'keeper.'"

—OnceUponaRomance.com

"Colleen is a master storyteller."

—Karen Kingsbury, bestselling author
of *Unlocked* and *Learning*

SILENT NIGHT, HOLY NIGHT

ALSO BY COLLEEN COBLE

HOPE BEACH NOVELS
Tidewater Inn
Rosemary Cottage
Seagrass Pier

UNDER TEXAS STARS NOVELS
Blue Moon Promise
Safe in His Arms

THE MERCY FALLS SERIES
The Lightkeeper's Daughter
The Lightkeeper's Bride
The Lightkeeper's Ball

LONESTAR NOVELS
Lonestar Sanctuary
Lonestar Secrets
Lonestar Homecoming
Lonestar Angel
All is Calm: A Lonestar
Christmas Novella (e-book only)

THE ROCK HARBOR SERIES
Without a Trace
Beyond a Doubt
Into the Deep
Cry in the Night
Silent Night: A Rock Harbor
Christmas Novella (e-book only)

THE ALOHA REEF SERIES
Distant Echoes
Black Sands
Dangerous Depths
Midnight Sea
Holy Night: An Aloha Reef
Christmas Novella (e-book only)

Alaska Twilight
Fire Dancer
Abomination
Anathema
Butterfly Palace

NOVELLAS INCLUDED IN:
Smitten
Secretly Smitten
Smitten Book Club

OTHER NOVELLAS
Bluebonnet Bride

SILENT NIGHT, HOLY NIGHT

A Colleen Coble Christmas Collection

COLLEEN COBLE

THOMAS NELSON
Since 1798

NASHVILLE   MEXICO CITY   RIO DE JANEIRO

Published in Nashville, Tennessee, by Thomas Nelson. Thomas Nelson is a registered trademark of HarperCollins Christian Publishing, Inc.

Thomas Nelson, Inc., titles may be purchased in bulk for educational, business, fund-raising, or sales promotional use. For information, please email SpecialMarkets@ThomasNelson.com.

Cover Design: James Hall
Cover Photography: Getty Images

**Library of Congress Cataloging-in-Publication
Data is available upon request.**

9780718001759

Printed in the United States of America

14 15 16 17 18 19 RRD 6 5 4 3 2 1

CONTENTS

SILENT NIGHT

ONE

THOUGH NO SHIPS CRUISED THE FROZEN WATERS OF Lake Superior, the foghorn bellowed its warning just outside Bree Matthews's lighthouse home window as she stood surveying the damage with the putty knife in her hand. Drifts of wallpaper lay strewn around the guest room. Her hands were gooey with old paste from the wet wallpaper, and her short, red curls felt sticky with it. Her search dog, Samson, a German shepherd/Chow mix, sulked just outside the door. She hadn't wanted paper in the dog's fur, but of course he hadn't understood her sharp tone.

She lifted a brow in her husband's direction. "Kade, what color do you think Lauri will like?" It helped to focus on pleasing her sister-in-law. Just a few months ago Bree had hoped to make this room into a nursery.

Kade spread out his broad hands and his genial grin came. "She's just going to be glad to get rid of the pink flowers." His new jeans hugged his hips, and the T-shirt showed off his muscles.

The three years they'd been married had flown by, and she loved him more with every passing day. Her failure to give him a baby made her heart ache every single day, and she was thirty-seven now. Her biological clock was ticking. Not that Kade complained. He loved Davy, her nine-year-old son from her first marriage. He'd been a true father to the fatherless. She imagined him holding a little boy with his thick dark hair and piercing blue eyes, and her heart gave a squeeze.

"Babe?" His hands come down on her shoulders.

She leaned into him, resting in his warmth and strength. "Sorry, I was woolgathering."

He smiled and brushed his lips across hers before glancing at the walls again. "How about we paint it a neutral color? Then you can decorate it however you like. Maybe a tan color you can team with blue or something."

"Sounds like a plan." Her words were much gayer than she felt, but she didn't want her pain to sadden him. Not today when the sun glinted on the snow and ice in a dazzling display. The Snow King put on his best robe in Michigan's Upper Peninsula.

Christmas would be here soon, and her entire family would be around the tree. Except her sister, Cassie, and Bree's mother. Bree still wasn't ready to see the woman who had made her childhood so miserable.

Samson rose in the doorway and turned toward the stairs. A low woof rumbled from his throat, a happy greeting reserved only for family. Davy was spending the night with his friend Timmy, so it couldn't be him.

"Who's there?" She laid down the putty knife and followed Kade into the hall. Samson ran down the stairs, his nails clicking on the hardwood.

A familiar figure stood at the bottom of the stairs. Dressed in a lavender ski jacket, Kade's sister, Lauri, stooped to rub Samson's head before slanting a smile toward them. Her light-brown hair was in a ponytail, and her slim-fitting jeans showed her youthful figure to advantage. Her dog, Zorro, a border collie mix, wagged his tail and woofed, then touched noses with Samson.

Bree smiled and started down the steps. "Lauri, we weren't expecting you until Christmas. I thought your semester didn't end for another two weeks."

"I wanted to surprise you. Don't come down. I'll bring my stuff to my room."

Surprise them. Bree feared what that might mean. The twenty-one-year-old had been a handful since her parents died when she was fifteen. Kade had done his best raising her from that point, but she liked her own way. All the time.

Kade stood aside as Lauri came up the stairs. "Uh, it's a mess, sis. We are redoing it as a surprise for you."

Lauri went to the doorway of her bedroom and gasped. "Holy cow. I can't sleep in here."

"No," Bree agreed. "We could put an air mattress in Davy's room, though. You can sleep in there. How long are you staying? We can try to get it done as quickly as possible, but with our schedules it will probably take at least a week."

"A week," Lauri echoed. "I can't sleep on the floor for a week."

"We have a new sofa," Bree said. "It might be more comfortable." When Lauri's eyes narrowed, she bit her lip. "Hey, how about if I call Martha? She doesn't have any guests right now. I'm sure she'd love to let you stay there."

"She'll be matchmaking," Lauri muttered. She dropped her army-green duffel bag on the floor. "But it looks like I don't have a choice." Samson and Zorro had followed closely at her heels, and Samson whined at her tone. She patted his head. "I'm not mad at *you*, boy."

Which by inference meant that she was mad at someone. Most likely her brother. She bristled every time Kade said or did anything. Though Bree hadn't been on the favored list lately either.

Bree suppressed a sigh. "We've got most of the wall-paper down. There's only one more wall to strip. Then I can wash it all down so Kade can repair the holes. Once that's all dry, I'll paint. You can pick out the color. We were just trying to decide what you'd like."

"Not pink." Lauri curled her lip.

"Of course not," Bree said. "Maybe a nice tan?"

Lauri shrugged. "We'll see. I sure wasn't expecting this mess."

"And we weren't expecting *you*," her brother said. "Lauri, it's time you grew up and showed a little appreciation. We wanted you to have a nice room when you came home. Bree has worked hard every day at her job, then she's come home and stripped wallpaper. It's a hard job, in case you were wondering."

Lauri had the grace to look ashamed. "Sorry, Bree. I didn't mean to sound ungrateful. It's been a long day."

Bree smiled, determined to turn the situation into a good one. "It sure has. Let me call Martha. Kade can help you carry in your things. Do you have more stuff in your car?"

"Yeah, but some of it can stay there until my room is ready."

Something in her tone caught Bree's attention. "There's something you're not telling us. And school isn't scheduled to be let out for two weeks. You didn't quit school, did you?"

Lauri's blue eyes flickered. "It's boring."

Kade pressed his lips together. "You're going right back, young lady. I didn't pay all that money for you to quit so close to graduation."

"I don't know what I want to do with my life," Lauri said. "I don't want to be an accountant for the rest of my life."

Kade's eyes narrowed. "You're good at it. You've always loved numbers. You only have one more semester. What did you tell the dean?"

She bit her lip. "I've got strep."

"For real or are you making it up?" Kade demanded.

"You want a doctor's slip?" Lauri dug in her purse and extracted a bottle. "Antibiotics, see? The nurse said I needed to rest." She glanced into her room. "Though it doesn't look like I'll be able to do that here."

Bree dug her cell phone out of the pocket of her jeans. "I'll take care of you, Lauri."

She placed the call to her next-door neighbor who assured her there was plenty of room for Lauri in the empty bed-and-breakfast. Another call beeped in her ear, and after thanking Martha, she hastily switched calls.

Mason Kaleva, the town sheriff, was on the other call. "Grab Samson and get out here. Some idiot in a parachute jumped out over Ottawa Forest and hasn't been seen since."

"On my way."

The woods had a fairy-tale appearance with thick clumps of snow bending the evergreen boughs low to the ground. Bree's breath fogged in front of her face as she paused to figure out where to head next. The sunset came quickly this time of year in the U.P. Her legs ached from tramping through the foot of freshly fallen snow in her snowshoes, and her stomach rumbled.

His tail wagging, Samson pressed his nose against her gloved hand. She answered his need and rubbed her palm over his head. "Good boy."

Her search-and-rescue partner and best friend, Naomi O'Reilly, eyed the shadows in the woods. "Going to be dark soon."

Naomi was Martha Heinonen's daughter, though they looked nothing alike. Naomi was slim and attractive with light-brown hair and blue eyes that were always smiling. She was married to the owner of the Ace Hardware store in Rock Harbor. Her small son was a toddler, and she was raising her husband's two children from a previous marriage.

They'd been searching for the missing parachutist for six hours. Bree feared he'd been killed. The trees
crowded close together here in the deep woods off Lake
Superior's icy waters, and there would have been no safe
place to land.

"Another hour or so. If he survived, he won't last the
night without shelter. It's supposed to get to thirty below
tonight." Bree's face stung from the cold, and she would
have to pull on a ski mask soon, but she hated to turn
back when they had to be close.

Samson and Naomi's dog, Charley, a golden retriever,
were both tired from the long day. She dug out food from
her pack and fed them, then ate a handful of pistachios
herself. Naomi refused her offer of nuts and munched on a
cheese stick instead. Neither of the women had stopped for
more than a snack in the last six hours.

Naomi blew into her cupped palms. "I don't know
why anyone would be parachuting in this weather. He's a
college student in Houghton. Maybe it was a dare. Who
knows?"

As if in answer to her question, Bree's satellite tele-
phone signaled an incoming call, and she unzipped it
from its pack to answer. "Bree Matthews."

Kade was on the other end. "They found the guy. He
didn't survive, though, I'm sorry to say."

Bree's eyes filled, and she gave Naomi a thumbs-down.

Her friend winced and slumped where she sat. This kind of outcome always depressed them. At least the dogs wouldn't have to feel the failure.

"It's going to take us a couple of hours to get back to the Jeep," she told Kade. "Do you know what happened to the parachutist?"

"The guy wanted to get into the marines, so he talked a friend into taking him up in the plane to practice jumping into foliage."

Such a waste. "I wonder if Lauri knew him."

"I didn't mention it to her. She dropped her stuff at Martha's, then went to town."

Bree frowned. "She's supposed to be resting."

"You believed her story?" Kade's laugh had an edge.

"She showed us the prescription." Though now that she thought of it, Bree hadn't looked at the name of the drug. "Get some food she likes and have it around, would you?"

"Maybe pizza. Be careful, babe. Get out of there as quickly as you can. The temperature is falling fast."

"I will. See you soon." Bree stowed the phone back in its case and told Naomi what Kade had said. "Ready to go home, Samson?"

The dog's tail swished faster, and he barked and ran in circles around her. She and Naomi donned their backpacks again and began to retrace their steps.

Something crashed through the brush to their right, and Bree assumed it was a deer until she saw a flash of lavender in the fading light. "Who's there?" A whimper answered her, and she moved closer to the quivering branches that hid the figure she couldn't quite make out.

Bree parted the evergreen branches to reveal a familiar figured crouched in the snow. "Lauri, what on earth are you doing out here?"

Her sister-in-law lay huddled in her lavender coat. The hood on the jacket was up, and the fur surrounded a face white with fatigue and cold. Bree didn't like the look of Lauri's skin. She might even have some frostbite.

Bree crouched beside her and touched her shoulder. "Are you hurt?"

Lauri wetted her lips and relief lit her face when she looked up. She accepted Bree's hand and stood. "I feel funny." She swayed where she stood, and her words were a little slurred.

"Exposure," Naomi mouthed.

Bree nodded and poured hot coffee from the Thermos. She made Lauri take three sips before more questioning. Naomi pulled out a thermal blanket and wrapped it around Lauri, then the women walked with her around the clearing. Color began to come back into Lauri's face.

"What are you doing out here?" Bree asked.

Lauri took another sip of coffee, then cupped her gloved hands around the steaming metal mug. "I was meeting Garrick. He was supposed to parachute in by the lake." She gestured vaguely at Little Piney Lake behind her. "I've been waiting for hours and he never came."

Bree's eyes widened. Garrick. The young man they'd been looking for. Should she tell Lauri now or get her to town before revealing what had happened? She wished Kade were here. He was always a rock they both leaned on.

Lauri's face crumpled when Bree didn't answer. "He's dead, isn't he? I felt it here." She put her hand over her heart. Tears rolled down her cheeks and she hiccoughed. "He can't be dead. I needed to find out . . ." She closed her mouth and inhaled.

Bree couldn't lie to her. "I'm sorry, honey, but yes. Naomi and I have been searching for him. He didn't make it." She put her arm around Lauri and hugged her. Lauri was tense, taut as a rubber band.

"Did they find his belongings too?"

Belongings? "I don't know anything about that." Something in the young woman's manner struck Bree as wrong. Maybe it was the way her gaze darted away, then back again. Or how fast her tears had dried. Lauri's bright blue eyes were cloud-free now. And tear-free.

Lauri's cheeks gained more color. "Where was he

found?" She sounded more alert, and her words were no longer slurred.

Bree turned back toward the path. "Kade didn't say. Not close, though, or we would have heard the commotion and seen lights. How did you get clear out here?"

Lauri pointed. "I brought Kade's snowmobile. I'd offer you a ride, but there are two of you and the dogs too. I didn't bring the sidecar. Thanks for telling me about Garrick."

Bree grabbed her arm. "The wind will make your hypothermia worse. Warm up a little more before you ride it back to town."

Lauri pulled out of her grip. "I'm fine. I need to get to town."

Bree knew better than to try to stop her again. Lauri could be a bull. The girl labored through the snow toward the frozen lake. Moments later the engine of a snowmobile roared.

Naomi harrumphed. "What's going on, Bree? First she says she's sick, then she goes traipsing around the woods in twenty-below temperatures."

"There's something odd about this," Bree said. "I'm going to have Kade talk to her."

Two

BREE WAS SO TIRED SHE COULD BARELY TRUDGE
through the drifts to her front porch. The lamppost by
the snow-covered brick path illuminated her way to the
lighthouse. Kade had turned on the Fresnel lens, though
there were no ships offshore, not with the lake frozen
over from this year's early and extreme cold.

She'd been tired a lot lately and had even made an
appointment with the doctor to see if maybe she had
mono. Samson hung back as well, almost too tired to
wag his tail when the door opened and Kade called to
him. The dog mustered the energy to dash past her and
disappear inside the beckoning warmth of their home.

At the sight of her husband's stocky frame, Bree
went up the steps with a burst of fresh energy. She was
starved and ready for Kade's support.

He draped his muscular arm around her. "You look beat, babe."

She leaned into the warmth of his embrace. "I'm pretty tired."

"Mason is on his way." He shut the door behind them and helped her out of her coat, then hung it in the hall closet. "The coffee's fresh."

The coffee's aroma perked her up. Her stomach cramped with hunger. Pistachios didn't go very far. "Did you save me any pizza?"

He kissed her, his lips warm and tender. "I brought home one just for you. Lots of pepperoni."

Elvis sang softly in the background from the surround-sound speakers in the living room. The tenseness in Bree's muscles relaxed as Kade led her to the sofa, then went to get her some coffee and pizza.

His dark eyes examined her with care when he returned with a tray. "It wasn't your fault, Bree."

Her fingers curled around the hot cup, and she sipped the coffee before answering, "I know."

The coffee was good and strong, laced with cream. She savored the heat on her tongue. The fire crackled and spread warm fingers toward her that she relished.

A knock came, then the front door opened, and a gust of wind rattled the panes. "I bet that's Mason." Kade stepped into the hall.

Mason Kaleva came into the living room behind

Kade. The sheriff was a burly man with dark curly hair. He was in his early forties and was married to Hilary, the town mayor and Bree's sister-in-law once upon a time. The families had stayed close even after her first husband's death, and Bree had always been thankful Kade accepted her ties to the Nicholls family.

Weariness lined Mason's weathered face. He nodded at Kade's offer of coffee, then dropped into the armchair by the fireplace. "Nasty business today. Poor guy didn't have a chance. Died upon impact with a tree."

Bree absorbed the news, then nodded. At least Garrick hadn't suffered in the cold waiting for help that never arrived. If only she could have told Kade about this in private.

She waited to speak until her husband returned with food and drink for Mason. She patted the sofa beside her, and Kade sat and put his arm around her.

She put down her coffee. "Lauri was out there. She said she was supposed to pick up Garrick after his jump. According to her, he was planning on landing at Little Piney Lake."

Kade stiffened and took his arm away. "So that's what she's doing here. I thought her story about why she'd come here sounded off."

"Did you hear her come in with the snowmobile?" Bree asked.

He shook his head. "I must have been in town

getting the pizza. I saw she'd been here and gone. Her boots were by the door. I tried to call her cell to see if she wanted pizza, but she never answered."

Mason stretched out his legs toward the fire. "If Little Piney Lake was his target, he missed it by miles. He landed near Big Piney."

A good fifteen miles to the west. Bree set her plate of pizza on the end table. "She asked about his belongings but didn't explain why."

Mason shrugged out of his heavy coat and tossed it on the floor by the fire. "He didn't have a pack or anything that we found. Just his jumpsuit and parachute. The jumpsuit was made of some special material that was supposed to keep him warm, but if he'd been stuck out there all night, I doubt it would have helped him much."

She leaned forward. "Why would he parachute into the woods? It's hard to hit a clearing when the wind is as high as it's been."

"He might not have heard the wind was supposed to pick up this afternoon." Mason took a sip of the hot coffee and stared into the fireplace flames for a moment. "I'll have some deputies look around tomorrow. By the time we found the poor guy, it was getting dark. We didn't know there was anything else to find. Or you could see if Samson can find anything. I'll have one of my deputies get a piece of his clothing from the morgue."

Bree nodded. "Maybe Lauri can tell you what he was doing out there in the winter."

"I could stop over there and talk to her. Normally I wouldn't bother her tonight, but it sounds like you're suspicious there might be something illegal going on."

Smuggling was not uncommon this close to the Big Sea Water, also known as Lake Superior. Boats brought in prescription drugs, illegal drugs, and even illegal aliens. It was more a sixth sense of something wrong than any actual clue Bree could point to. She prayed Lauri wasn't involved in something bad.

"I'll go with you if you're going." Bree reached her hand out to Kade, who wore a stricken expression. His fingers closed around hers.

"We've got a few minutes. I'm famished." Mason tucked into his pizza and coffee with gusto.

Bree did the same, though her initial appetite had left her. Kade wouldn't let her leave if she didn't eat, though, so she managed to get down a piece of pizza and her coffee. The fatigue dragging at her muscles lifted when Mason excused himself to stop at the restroom.

When Kade grabbed his coat, Bree put her hand on his arm. "I don't think you should come, honey. You're too mad. She's more likely to talk to me."

His mouth was tight, and he shook his head. "I'll make her tell me what's going on."

"Let me try a little sugar first. If that doesn't work, you can talk to her. Let's see what she tells me." She smiled to soften the words, but Kade didn't smile back.

"I can't remember the last time I saw a real smile." His words were soft. "Maybe not since you lost the baby. But you don't talk about it. Why not?"

She winced, knowing he was more than a little right. "I want a baby, Kade. The longing never leaves."

"You know I do too. But we have Dave even if God doesn't bless us with a baby. We're happy, aren't we? Aren't the three of us enough?"

She wanted to smooth the worry from his brow with a yes, but her heart clenched at the thought that she would never hold Kade's baby in her arms.

She turned toward the door. "I'll be back as quickly as I can."

The wind howled along the eaves and whistled past the windows as Kade settled in front of the fireplace with his MacBook. The pain in Bree's eyes tore at his heart. The doctor couldn't find anything wrong with either of them.

He hadn't yet shown Bree the link he clicked now. Maybe she wasn't ready. Maybe he wasn't either, but he fingered his cell phone, tempted to call the number on his screen. The adoption process would be long and hard. Costly too, but he'd been tucking away money for several months now. Mason's wife would know more than he did about all of this. It would be better to start there. He brought up her number and placed the call.

"Kade?" Hilary's voice held curiosity. "Is everything all right? Mason texted me that he was out of the woods."

"He is. I have something personal to talk to you about. But I have to ask you not to say anything to Bree yet."

There was a long pause on the phone. "Well, that's rather surprising. I thought you two had the perfect marriage and shared everything."

Hilary always knew exactly where to stick the knife. He cleared his throat. "We do, but I want to wait until the right time to talk to her about this, and I need some information first."

"All right. But don't make me keep the secret for long. Bree is my sister-in-law. I wouldn't want her to hold anything against me."

Once upon a time, the two had been on edge with one another, but life had softened Hilary, and she tended to be protective of Bree. Kade couldn't fault her for that when he felt the same way.

"She won't be mad at you. It's nothing like that."

"So how can I help you?"

There was no way to segue into the topic with any finesse. "I wondered if you had any recommendations about adoption. What agency or attorney? How long does it take and how much does it cost? That kind of thing."

Her gasp was sharp on the other end. "Adoption? That was the last thing I expected. You two have Davy."

"But we'd like a houseful of kids. You know she's miscarried."

"I know how painful that is." Her voice was tight.

She did know too. She and Mason had tried to have a baby for years until they'd adopted Lauri's baby daughter when she became pregnant at sixteen. For all he knew, they were still trying to have one, though Hilary was nearing forty by now. Not impossible, though.

He cleared his throat past the pain constricting it. "The doctor says to relax and not worry, but of course we do."

"Of course." Her tone turned brisk. "There's a very good attorney in Houghton. We used him to finalize Zoe's adoption, and he handles private adoptions. Have you thought about foster care? Sometimes a child is placed in your home who becomes adoptable, and you would be the first in line."

He winced. "I don't think she could stand to lose another baby. Not after Olivia."

About a year ago, he and Bree had cared for a baby who'd been discovered when a stolen baby ring had settled in town, and Bree had taken care of the infant for a while. When her parentage was traced and she was given back to her mother, Bree had cried for weeks.

"Of course. Well, then try my attorney, Philip Masters. Hang on and I'll get his number."

Kade grabbed a pen and paper, then wrote it down when she came back on the line and rattled it off. "How long does it take?"

"It depends on what you want. The wait is much shorter if you're willing to take a baby of a different race or one with some health problems. Are you?"

"I—I don't know. This will all be very new to both of us. We'll need to talk it over." He would be fine with a mixed-race child and suspected Bree would be too. And he had good insurance, so if a child had some health problems, they'd deal with that as well. "What about a Caucasian child?"

"Could be years."

Years. He thought about the long wait for a call that might never come. "I see. And the costs?"

"Expensive. You'll need to pay for the baby's delivery and hospital costs. It's also usual to pay the mother's living expenses for a while. Count on twenty thousand at least, but it could run as high as forty thousand."

His gut clenched. Hilary might as well have told him it would be a million dollars. Even though he'd been promoted in the park service, he didn't have that kind of money laying around. His gaze swept the comfortable living room. They might be able to get a second mortgage on their lighthouse home. They'd worked hard to pay off the mortgage and had paid cash for improvements.

He exhaled. "I guess this is pretty preliminary. I have no idea if Bree would be willing to talk about it. She's pretty set on having a baby herself."

"Sometimes that doesn't work out." Hilary's voice held pain. "Have you heard from Lauri lately?"

"Funny you should mention Lauri. She showed up today. Just up and left two weeks before the semester ended."

Hilary didn't answer for a few long moments. "I've been thinking it might be time to tell Zoe the truth. I want it to be so natural that she never blames me and Mason for withholding information from her. We've talked about the fact that she's adopted, though of course she doesn't really understand it."

Once upon a time, Hilary would have tried to go to her grave keeping that secret. The woman had changed so much.

He walked to the window and looked out onto the

moonlit snow. "I think that's wise. I can talk to Lauri about it."

Who knew how his volatile kid sister would react? She seemed to have been able to completely let go of little Zoe without a qualm. She was older now, though. At some point he expected regrets to begin to form.

The last thing he wanted was to see a division develop in the family because of this.

THREE

BREE STOMPED HER FEET ON THE MAT, THEN SHOOK THE snow from her jacket before handing it to Martha Heinonen. Mason had already shucked his boots and coat and stood in his stocking feet on the gleaming oak floors of the entry to the elegant bed-and-breakfast.

Though it was nearly eight, Naomi's mother still wore a blue dress and heels. Martha played up her resemblance to Queen Elizabeth when she was in her sixties, even to the way she wore her hair. The dress matched her cornflower-blue eyes too. She'd never remarried after her husband died when Naomi was five.

"Bree, you look half frozen," Martha scolded. "Come in by the fire and tell me why you're out here when you should be resting after today's ordeal. Mason, you should know better than to get her out in this."

No one could stand up to Martha, least of all the mild-mannered sheriff. He exchanged a glance with Bree, then followed Martha to the living room, where a fire blazed in the marble hearth. A cinnamon-scented candle flickered on the mantel. Bree had always loved this room. She felt as much a part of the Heinonen family as her best friend Naomi herself.

When she settled on the overstuffed sofa, Martha tucked a garnet chenille throw around her. "Cuddle up in that and get warm. Tea?"

"I just had coffee." Bree patted the seat beside her. "We wanted to ask you some questions."

Martha sat beside Bree, then picked up her crochet project from a needlework bag on the floor. "Me?" She plunged a blue afghan needle into the yarn and began to loop it.

The natural-colored afghan was nearly done, and it matched dozens of others Bree had seen Martha make. At their wedding she and Kade were the recipients of one that had been embroidered with their names.

Bree straightened the throw on her lap. "How did Lauri act when she got here? Did she say anything about why she was here and where she was going when she left?"

Martha's blue eyes narrowed. "You know Lauri. She never tells you anything."

Bree sighed. "Naomi and I saw her out in the woods. She said she was there to pick up the parachuter who died today. So she didn't say where she was going when she left here? She stopped at our place, then said she was going out. Kade didn't question her. You know how guys are."

Martha smiled and moved the crochet hook through the yarn without looking at Bree. "She said she was here photographing someone learning to skydive. She's working on a thesis project for school. Or so she told me."

Bree frowned. "Weird. That doesn't sound like any kind of accounting class. Maybe it's for an elective."

Mason still stood warming his hands by the fire. His expression held the same skepticism Bree was sure resided on her face. Her gut feeling was rarely wrong, and it appeared her sixth sense hadn't led her astray this time either.

"Did she appear upset when she came in tonight?" he asked.

Martha frowned. "She was fairly quiet and arrived a bit late for supper. I warmed up some stew for her, though. She ate, then went to her room."

"Would you mind telling her I'd like to speak with her?" Mason asked.

"Of course." Martha put her yarn and needle aside, then hustled toward the door.

"What do you make of that story?" Bree asked as Martha's steps faded up the stairway.

"There could be some reasonable explanation. Maybe she was seeing this guy on the sly and didn't want anyone to know, especially Kade. Or he could have asked her to pick him up when he found out she was in the area."

"Or it really was for some kind of class project. There's a skydiving club in Houghton." She'd seen the group out on occasion. It had ceased for a while when they lost their plane, but a few years later was up and flying again.

Two sets of footsteps came down the stairs. Bree's smile was firmly in place when Lauri followed Martha into the living room. Lauri's brown hair, now out of the ponytail, hung halfway down her back, and she looked even younger and more vulnerable in the soft glow of the lights. A little color had returned to her cheeks.

Her eyes widened when she saw Bree. "I thought the sheriff wanted to see me."

"I do," Mason said from his position by the fireplace.

Lauri's hands curled into fists at her side, but her smile stayed in place. "Is this about Garrick?" Her blue eyes flickered warily from him to Bree then back.

Mason fixed her with a stare. "I shouldn't have had to track you down here. We had no idea someone was supposed to pick him up in the woods. Bree informs me that you indicated he planned to land on Little Piney."

Lauri took a step back. "I don't really remember what I said. I was babbling from the cold, I think. He was actually supposed to land on Big Piney, and I got confused and then lost." She didn't look at Bree.

Bree managed to hide her indignation. "That's not what you told me, Lauri. You said you'd been waiting out there for hours, and he never showed up. And that reminds me. You were with me when I got the call to search for him. If you were supposed to pick him up, why weren't you in the woods then?"

"He told me to get him at three. So that's what I planned to do. I didn't know who you were searching for. You grabbed your ready pack and left with no details." She pressed her lips together. "I really don't know anything about this. Garrick was just a friend who asked me to do him a favor."

Bree knew there was more. "As in boyfriend?"

Lauri shrugged. "As in a boy who is a friend."

Bree's hands curled into fists under the throw. If he was a friend, or even something more, she would have expected Lauri to be upset, instead she seemed more angry. Why was she lying?

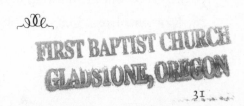

31

Suomi Café overlooked Lake Superior from its perch on the steep slope of Kitchigami Street. Named for the Finnish word for Finland, the humble restaurant offered no exterior hint of the culinary delights inside. Just thinking of the possible menu choices made Bree's mouth water.

She glanced around when she entered, but Lauri hadn't arrived, though she'd told Bree on the phone this morning she would meet her at nine.

The head waitress, Molly, a full tray in her skinny arms, nodded to her. In her forties, Molly was a whirlwind of activity every time Bree came in. It was no wonder she carried not an ounce of spare flesh on her thin frame.

She set the steamy plates before her customers, then stopped beside Bree. "Just you?"

"Lauri and Hilary are joining me."

Molly led her to a corner booth that looked out onto a snowy courtyard. "What will you have, eh? The *panukakkua* just came out of the oven."

Panukakkua. The thought of the custard pancake dripping with hot raspberry sauce brought a Pavlovian response from Bree. "You know my weakness," Bree said, nodding. "And coffee."

"You got it." Molly tucked the order pad into a pocket of her apron and went to the kitchen.

Moments later Hilary, her blond hair in a neat bob,

came toward the table with purposeful steps. "Where's Lauri?"

"On her way, I hope." When Hilary sat down on the other side of the booth, Bree eyed her. "You're sure about this? I didn't say anything to Lauri about you being here. Or what you wanted. I'd rather it come from you."

"That's fine. I know just what I want to say. And it's perfect that it's Christmas."

Bree didn't get a chance to ask her what she meant because the bell over the door jingled, and Lauri approached with a hesitant expression.

She slid into the seat beside Bree. "Hey, Hilary. I didn't know you were going to be here." She shot an accusatory glance Bree's way.

"I thought we'd meet on neutral ground, so to speak," Hilary said. "You look well, Lauri. How is school?"

"Fine." Lauri kept her head down and mumbled her order at Molly when the waitress appeared with her pad and pencil.

When Molly left, Hilary leaned forward. "I'm sure you are wondering why I want to see you."

"Yeah, that thought crossed my mind." Lauri finally raised her head. Her blue eyes were wary.

"I want to tell Zoe you're her mother."

Lauri bolted from her seat. "What?"

Bree reached over and grabbed her hand. "Sit back down and listen. Hilary's plan makes a lot of sense."

Lauri sat back in the booth, her back stiff. "Why would you want to do this? Don't you realize how hard this is on me?" Her voice broke. "Every time I see Zoe I regret everything in my life. I messed up bad. I don't want her to suffer for what I did. What if she thinks I just threw her away? She's too young to hear this." She shook her head vehemently. "No."

Bree touched Lauri's hand again, but the girl snatched it away. "Hilary, do you want to explain?"

Hilary stirred honey in her tea. "If we tell her now, when it's not a big deal and she really doesn't understand it, there will never be some big, shocking revelation that upsets her life. We'll tell her you were too young to raise a baby, and we had a room all ready for her. That we all love her very much. That you're one kind of mommy and I'm another kind. Gradually, she'll come to understand."

"I don't like it." Lauri's voice was panicked. "And we both signed a paper for a closed adoption. I don't want her to ever know. Right now she likes me. I don't want her to hate me."

Hilary pressed her lips together and said nothing as a large party of hunters came past talking loudly about their morning. When the hubbub faded, she reached over and took Lauri's hand in an uncharacteristically gentle gesture. Lauri didn't pull away. "I know that's what we agreed on, but Mom made me see how wrong it was. A child can never have too much love."

Tears leaked from Lauri's eyes. "This isn't the right thing to do."

Bree had seen the way Lauri stared longingly at little Zoe. And who wouldn't? The little girl was darling, with Lauri's soft brown hair and big blue eyes. Bree hadn't expected Lauri to disagree.

Hilary withdrew her hand and leaned back. "I want to tell her at Christmas. I have it all planned. You can get her a present and we'll let her open it on Christmas Eve at Bree's. I'll tell her it's from her younger mommy and run through what I just said. She's so little that she won't absorb much of it, but over time she'll come to understand. It will be a natural progression over the years."

"A present? You mean like a doll?" Lauri swallowed hard, then shook her head. "I just said no. I don't want to talk about it anymore."

Lauri's statement said so much. Bree could imagine her pausing in the toy aisle and looking at the dolls with little Zoe in mind.

"Lauri, we have to talk about this. I know you love her."

"I do love her, Hilary. Don't ever think I don't. I want what's best for her, but this isn't it."

"Of course you love her. Who wouldn't?" Hilary fell silent when Molly brought their breakfast.

They said nothing more for a few minutes as they began to eat their food. Bree felt a warmth toward Lauri, a sense of sorrow for the pain Lauri must be feeling.

The bell on the door jingled again, and Kade stepped into the restaurant and came toward them. "Babe, Mason wants us to go on that search. You ready? I've got Samson on the snowmobile."

Bree took one final bite and another gulp of coffee. "Let's go." She glanced at Lauri. "Would you mind getting Davy after school?"

"I'd be glad to. I'll take him cross-country skiing."

"Thanks." Bree watched Lauri leave. Would she be willing to do what was best for Zoe?

FOUR

THE SUN SHONE WEAKLY IN A PALE-BLUE SKY BUT DID little to warm the frigid air. Bree clung to Kade's waist on the snowmobile. His bulk shielded her from the worst of the wind, and she rested her cheek on his broad back. Samson wore a doggy smile on his face from his secure spot in the sidecar. The engine's roar bounced off the trees lining the narrow, snow-covered road, and Bree was glad for the muffling effect of her earmuffs and hood.

She pointed and spoke in her husband's ear. "Up ahead."

Traveling by snowmobile made getting to the spot where Mason had found Garrick much easier. The moisture from the fresh snow would help Samson sniff out any of the young man's belongings. The snowmobile path veered from the road into the woods, which was both good and bad. The trees blocked the wind, but the shade took the temperature down a few degrees. Her fingers were already numb, in spite of her insulated mittens. Samson didn't seem bothered by the cold. There was space for him to huddle out of the wind, but instead he sat erect with his ears up.

Kade had seemed quiet last night. She'd been glad to have something to think about besides her failure to get pregnant again. Did he blame her for the miscarriage? Though she hadn't fallen, she'd been her usual active self and had continued to train the dogs and search for missing persons.

She ducked behind Kade's back to escape a low-hanging evergreen branch. The trees began to thin a bit, and she caught a glimpse of the frozen surface of Big Piney Lake. Lauri had been right about that, at least. Somehow she'd heard Garrick had been found here instead of Little Piney. It was possible she'd misunderstood where she was supposed to pick up her friend, but Bree was convinced there was more to it than that.

The snowmobile slowed at the edge of the lake, then Kade parked the machine. The sudden cessation of the rumble made her ears ring. She dismounted, then got Samson out of the sidecar before retrieving the paper bag that held a piece of Garrick's clothing. Two cardinals, bright splashes of red in a white landscape, regarded her from a bush before fluttering to a higher branch when they realized they had Samson's attention.

She diverted him by letting him sniff the scent bag. His tail stiffened and he looked alert.

"Ice is a good eighteen inches deep," Kade said. "Mason said he was found on the far side, and it would be faster to take the snowmobile. I wanted to make sure the ice was safe."

Her search dog wasn't a bloodhound but an air scenter. He worked in a Z pattern, scenting the air until he could catch a hint of the one scent he sought. Samson's tail stiffened, and he turned and raced toward the lake.

"He's caught it!" Bree said, running after her dog.

Samson bounded through the deep snow with a happy bark. He loved it out here, and even high drifts failed to dampen his enthusiasm. The dog headed straight for a tree twenty feet away. Its trunk was partly in the lake, and its branches leaned out over the edge of the frozen water. A rope hung from the thickest branch, probably put there by adventurous teenaged boys. Ice encrusted the rope's surface.

Samson stopped and grabbed a stick in his mouth, then struggled back to Bree with his tail wagging. The snow came nearly up to his belly.

"Good boy," she crooned. "You found it."

Kade was on her heels. He glanced around the area. "I don't see anything."

"Me neither, but Samson says it's here." She craned her neck. "Maybe it's in the tree." She grasped the low-hanging evergreen tree limb and tried to pull herself onto the branch. "Give me a hand."

"Let me climb it. I don't want you to fall." He tested the limb and it bent. "I'm not sure it will support my weight, though." He knelt. "Climb on my shoulders, and see if you can find anything that way."

She did as her husband said. Her head whacked the nearest branch when he moved, and she felt something shift. "Hang on." Perched on his broad shoulders, she began to part the pine branches above her. The pine and snow were so thick it was hard to see, so she removed her mittens and felt along the pine needles with her fingers. The scent of pine mingled with the fresh, cold smell of snow in an aroma that was all North Woods. Magpies scolded from their perch high above her head.

She was beginning to think Samson had misread the scent when her hand touched something that felt like rough canvas. It was on a branch far above her head and she couldn't see. Her fingers closed around what felt like a strap and she tugged at it. A shower of snow fell on her head and Kade's as well. When she flinched, the movement unbalanced her husband. He reeled back, his arms grasping for something, but his grab at a branch missed.

Her fingers were still curled around her discovery, but that was no source of stability either as a bag left the branch where it had been perched. As it landed on her head, she began to slip from Kade's shoulders. The next thing she knew she was in a snow drift on top of Kade.

"If you wanted a kiss, all you had to do was ask." His blue eyes were smiling, and he carefully brushed the snow from her hair. "You're not hurt, are you?"

"Only my pride." She grinned and wrapped her arms around him. "So how about that kiss?"

~♃~

Mason's office smelled of stale coffee and old floors when Kade dropped the bag onto the sheriff's desk. The backpack was black, gray, and well used. The weather hadn't done it any favors. "I think the zipper is broken."

"Good job," Mason said. "Did you try to unzip it?" He opened a desk drawer and took out a box of latex gloves, then put on a pair.

Kade pulled a chair closer to the desk for Bree and pointed. "Yeah, but it's stuck and I didn't want to do any damage until you got a chance to look at it."

Bree dropped into the chair while Kade dragged

another one near. Samson leaned his head against her knee, and she rubbed his ears. "Have you found the pilot who dropped Garrick off?"

Mason yanked on the pack, then gave up. "Not yet. No one really noticed the plane. The two hikers who reported the incident saw Garrick falling straight down into the trees. I think they were too shocked to look for the plane. Every airport I've checked has reported no skydivers going up. So whoever the pilot was, he didn't file the right flight plan."

Kade glanced at his wife, who was looking pensive. He knew she was worried about Lauri's involvement. So was he. His sister was being even more secretive than usual, and he struggled to figure out her role in this.

"So what's next?" Bree leaned back in her chair.

Samson huffed with indignation at her neglect, then settled on the floor by her feet. Kade dug a treat from his pocket and gave it to the dog.

Mason shrugged. "We keep digging. I'm going to bring Lauri in for official questioning."

Kade's gut tightened. "Is that really necessary?"

"I need to know how she knew the deceased." Mason studied the bag. "She knows more than she's telling. I think we all know that."

Kade wanted to object, but it would be useless. He could only pray Lauri was innocent of any wrongdoing. "What do you know about Garrick?"

"He was a civil engineering student at Michigan Tech. In his last year of a scholarship with his senior year still to go."

"Smart guy, then. Such a tragedy." Kade glanced at the backpack. "Can we cut that open or something?"

"Yeah." Mason dug in his desk drawer and pulled out a utility knife. Once he slid out the razor blade, he cut the fabric along the side of the zipper. His face darkened when he looked inside. "I don't like this." He pulled out rope, duct tape, and a syringe.

Kade stared at the items. "It's like he was planning on subduing someone."

"Anything else in there?" Bree asked.

Mason looked inside, then ran his hand around the bottom. "What's this?" The piece of paper in his hand was water stained and crumpled. He unfolded it and a necklace fell out. The delicate gold chain looked worn. Tiny scratches burnished the heart locket.

"Wait a minute," Bree said. "Can I see that necklace?" She reached for gloves like Mason wore.

Mason dropped the necklace into her outstretched palm and she studied it. "There's something about this . . ." She snapped her fingers. "I remember now. There was a missing girl in Houghton. Her parents said she wore a heart locket her grandmother had given her. She never took it off. We never did find her, but we found a hole where we think she fell through the ice."

Kade remembered the search. Bree had been quiet for two days afterward.

Mason glanced at the paper, then grimaced. "Recognize this number?" He held it up so they could read it. The name *Lauri* was followed by a phone number.

"That's Lauri's cell phone number," Kade admitted.

Bree glanced at him, her green eyes wide. "But that doesn't mean anything. She's already told us she was supposed to pick him up. Maybe he wrote down the number because he didn't know it. That corroborates her insistence he was just a friend. A boyfriend would know her number by heart."

Kade thanked her with his smile, though he could tell by Mason's expression he wasn't swayed. "You wouldn't think it would be on the bottom of the pack."

"It wasn't." Kade flipped the bag around so it was facing the right direction. "We cut it open on the bottom."

So Lauri's name and number were at the top of the satchel, within easy reach for Garrick to call for a pickup. He'd never had the chance.

Kade studied the items on Mason's desk again. "Anything in on the parachuting accident?"

Mason raised a brow. "We're investigating the possibility that someone tampered with the parachute."

"You mean—murder?" Bree exhaled and shook her head. "I'd rather believe it was a terrible accident."

"We won't know for a few more days. I've called in the state boys to help. The college wants this handled as quickly as possible too."

Bree glanced up at Kade, and he read the question in her eyes. "How about we check out the college? Ask around and see who his friends were, then the state police can question them." *Including Lauri.*

"I wouldn't turn down the help, not with the winter festival coming. I've got two deputies out this week with the flu too. But keep a low profile. State may not like me allowing you to poke around."

"Not a problem," Kade said. "It's early yet. We could be there by two."

At Kade's tone, Samson leaped to his feet and padded toward the door.

Mason scribbled a few lines on a piece of paper and thrust it into Kade's hands. "Call me if you run into trouble."

FIVE

PAULIE, KADE'S PET CARDINAL, CALLED TO THEM WHEN
they exited the sheriff's office. Bree was almost too pre-
occupied to notice Kade pause to dig in his pocket and
toss seeds to the bird. The bright-red bird hopped along
the snow and scooped up the offering.

Kade opened the truck door for her, and she slid in,
relaxing in the familiar scents of his vehicle. Mint gum
mixed with the scent of spicy cologne and the smell of
the metal cages behind the seat. If she looked, she knew
she'd see snowshoes and snacks back there too. Her husband practically lived in his truck as he patrolled the
Ottawa forest for the National Park Service.

Kade got in and turned the key. His jawline was
tight and grim. "I should be able to trust Lauri, but she's
proven her poor judgment more than once."

"Let's not jump to conclusions. There may be an innocent explanation." Bree leaned back as the truck rolled out of town.

Her cell phone rang, and she smiled at the music. "Always on My Mind" by Elvis was her ring tone for her sister who lived in Washington State. Cassie was working at a cranberry farm, helping them grow bigger and better fruit.

Bree answered the phone. "Hey, sis. What's up?"

"I was missing my big sister and guess what? I have time off for Christmas. Can I crash on your couch?"

"Oh my gosh, I haven't seen you in forever! How long can you stay?" They'd spent all their childhood apart, and Bree had longed to make up for lost time. Cassie was a busy professional, though, and they'd only been together a handful of times in the past two years.

She glanced at Kade. He grinned and gave her a thumbs-up. She chatted with her sister a few minutes, then put her cell phone away. "Cassie will be here for Christmas!"

"When's she coming?"

Bree couldn't stop smiling. "Christmas Eve. She can stay until after the first."

"We might need to ask Martha for a room. Depends on how long Lauri plans to stay."

Bree wanted them all close at hand. "Cassie said she

could crash on the sofa, but I hate to have her sleep there that long. What if we put two beds in Lauri's room? It's plenty big enough to share. Unless you think Lauri would object."

His jawline hardened. "Lauri objects to everything, but it's our house, and we can do what's best for our family. I think that's a great idea. Even two queen beds would fit. And the closet is big enough too. We can get another dresser as well."

The sunshine warmed the blacktop and began to melt the snow from the road's surface. She never tired of the winter wonderland where she lived.

"Are you doing okay, honey? We'll get this figured out. Lauri will grow up sometime."

Kade pressed his lips together. "I'm beginning to doubt that." He glanced at her out of the corner of his eye. "Now's as good a time as any to talk to you about something."

The gravity in his manner made her fingers curl into her palms. "Is something wrong?"

He gave her another glance, then looked back at the road as a large motor home lumbered around the curve, narrowed by snow drifts. "I've been thinking. What would you think about adopting a child?"

His question took her breath away. She looked at him, noticing she hadn't cut his hair lately. And he'd lost weight. From worrying about her? She wetted her lips. "Where is this coming from? You think we'll never have a baby?" She had to force the words out as if admitting it might happen would make it real. Acid churned in her stomach.

"We would have adopted Olivia if her mother hadn't been found. You wanted to keep her."

"I'd fallen in love with her from caring for her. You're talking about adopting some unknown child. I love children, you know that. But adoption is a big step."

"You don't sound totally against it."

"I'm not, but I'd like the chance to have our own baby." She pressed her hand against her stomach. Would a baby ever grow there again? Getting pregnant with Davy had seemed so easy, so natural. Why was it hard now?

"Can we agree to at least think about it? I talked to Hilary about it."

She inhaled sharply. "Oh, Kade, you didn't! That was pretty insensitive. She's going to pry into our business now."

He hunched his shoulders. "I want us to have a baby."

She bit her lip at his words. Was that censure? Did he blame her? "I'm not ready to give up on us yet. Adoptions are expensive. If we spend all our money on adopting a baby, what happens if I end up pregnant and we're tapped out from the adoption costs? I'd rather we didn't rush into anything."

He kept his eyes on the road and didn't look at her. "I'm not saying we rush into it. But let's open a dialogue."

Tears pricked the backs of her eyes at his curt tone. She'd always known he wanted a child. Everything in her longed to place a baby in his arms—*their baby*. Though she knew she could love any child, she wanted to give him a child that carried his genes. She wanted a little boy with his dark hair and kind manner she could carry beneath her heart.

She wanted to bring his smile back. "We can talk about it as long as you don't push me to decide right away. I want to see what the doctor has to say. We haven't tried all our options yet."

He shook his head. "You're talking about in vitro. It's expensive too and has no guarantees."

"No, there are never guarantees in life, but I want to at least try, Kade. I can't just give up without trying. One pass of in vitro is ten thousand dollars. Adoption can run much higher."

"But we'd be assured of a baby at the end of it."

She turned her head and gazed out the window. "Let's table this for now, okay? I'll think about it. I promise."

"Fine."

They said nothing more until they reached the outskirts of Houghton, but Bree's thoughts never slowed.

Houghton's downtown was built on a slope. Narrow side streets led to shops and cafes. After stopping for coffee, Kade drove to Michigan Tech. The university started in 1885 to train mining engineers. The campus now boasted many different majors and was rated one of the top colleges in the country. Kade had graduated from here himself.

They drove past the impressive campus to a side street where Garrick had rented an apartment with several friends. The blue paint barely clung to the two-story house, and the wood showed through the peeling layers in several spots. The porch and windows looked new, and the sidewalk appeared freshly poured. Two doors opened off the porch, presumably to different apartments.

"Which one?" he asked when they got out and stood on the street. They had left Samson in the truck and it was hard to ignore his whine.

Bree consulted the paper in her hand. "Apartment two."

The numbers on the old siding hung at an angle. He took Bree's arm and guided her to the brown door. Music blared from inside, the thump too distant to identify, and the scent of patchouli incense seeped from around the door's cracks. He pressed the doorbell, then rapped on the door's window for good measure.

"Coming," a male voice called from inside.

The young man who yanked open the door looked like he'd just gotten out of bed. His hair, dyed an impossible red tone, stood on end, and his hazel eyes were bleary. He wore a wrinkled yellow T-shirt and stained jeans. The scent of patchouli was stronger with the door open, and Kade smelled cinnamon rolls now too.

"Hello, I'm Kade Matthews, and this is my wife, Bree. You may have heard of her. She's the search-and-rescue worker who was out looking for Garrick Harper, your roommate."

"Cool." The young man stared at Bree. "I've seen your picture on the news."

"We wondered if we might ask you a few questions. We're trying to figure out what happened to Garrick."

"I guess so. I can't talk long, though. I have class in an hour." He stepped aside and allowed them to enter the narrow hall painted in electric green. A small dog raced to meet them, yapping furiously. It put its front paws on her leg.

Bree held out her hand, and the terrier sniffed before licking her fingers. She smiled. "You're a cutie." She straightened and glanced at the dog's owner. "What's your name?"

"Andy."

"Could we take a look at Garrick's room?" Kade asked.

Andy set his jaw. "Not without a warrant."

Bree shot Kade a quick look, then sent a placating smile Andy's way. "We wondered if you had any idea who took Garrick up in the plane. Do you know what he was doing?"

Andy shook his head. "Our schedules never meshed. I'd see him in passing and that was about it. You might ask the neighbor in the other apartment. Lauri Matthews. She talked to him quite a bit after she moved in."

Kade's jaw dropped, but he quickly hid his shock. Lauri lived next door? When had she moved and why? She hadn't said a word to him about this. "When did Lauri move in?"

"About a week ago. She was friends with that girl who went missing. Frannie Hastings."

The one Bree had searched for. Kade glanced over and saw Bree nod.

"As I recall, she went cross-country skiing and never came back," Bree said.

Andy picked up his dog. "Yeah, the search turned up her skis, but she was never found. They gave up after a week."

"My search dog, Samson, found those skis," Bree said. "We also found her backpack and an area where the ice had been broken through. The sheriff assumed she'd fallen in, though her body was never recovered."

Kade put his arm around her waist when he heard the pain in her voice. These bad outcomes always affected her. "Did you talk to Lauri when she moved in?"

Andy's eyes widened. "It just clicked you said your name was Matthews. Are you related?"

"My sister."

"And you didn't know she lived here?"

Kade shook his head. "She didn't mention it. So she and Garrick were friends? How close?"

Andy shrugged. "They hung out. I don't think they were going out or anything. She was always asking about Frannie."

Kade tried to remember if Lauri had mentioned Frannie. And when she went missing, as far as he knew, Lauri hadn't called to ask Bree's help. The authorities in Houghton had done that.

Andy shook his head. "I don't think she knew Frannie well but Garrick did. They were lab partners."

"Did Garrick skydive often?" Bree asked.

"Like I said, we didn't talk much." Impatience crept into his tone. "To tell you the truth, I was surprised to find out he was killed in that accident. I never went in his room so I didn't know skydiving was a hobby of his."

Strange that roommates could know so little about one another. Just past Andy's shoulder, Kade saw the living room with video games strewn around the tables and the floor in front of the fifty-two-inch television that was still on, frozen on what appeared to be a Spider-Man game of some kind. Most likely Andy was too busy playing games to talk to his roommate.

"Anything else you can tell us about Garrick?" Bree asked. "Anything at all? Jobs, hang outs, anything?"

Andy put the dog on the floor. "Like I said, I didn't know him very well. I'd ask Lauri."

"I intend to do just that," Kade said.

SIX

KADE CLOSED THE LIGHTHOUSE DOOR AGAINST THE cold wind blowing in off Lake Superior. "Lauri!" It smelled like freshly baked chocolate chip cookies.

Bree laid her hand on his arm. "Don't get mad. Let's give her a chance to explain."

He moved toward the closet and her hand fell away. "I want the best for her, but she exasperates the heck out of me."

Her green eyes were troubled. "I think your high standards make Lauri even more determined to be the wild child and show you she can go her own way."

So first she didn't like him calling Hilary, and now she was insinuating it was his fault Lauri didn't toe the line. He hung up his coat.

Lauri appeared in the doorway to the living room with Davy by her side and Zorro at her heels. "Is the house on fire?"

Kade's heart softened when he saw Davy. "No, but we have something to talk to you about. Son, we need to talk to your aunt in private. If you'll go load up your airplane, I'll take you out to fly it when we're done."

"Yeah!" The boy's grin was wide, and he took the steps to his bedroom two at a time.

Davy was nine now, and though he wanted to be called Dave, Bree found it hard not to use the old familiar name, though Kade found it easy. The boy's red hair needed a bit of a trim, and he'd grown two inches in this past year. He'd be a young man before they could blink.

The caution in Lauri's blue eyes broke Kade's heart. Maybe Bree was right, and he was too hard on his sister. Their parents had wanted so much for both of them, and he often felt he'd failed them. When they'd died, he'd known nothing about raising a teenage girl.

Bree slipped her arm around the young woman's waist and turned her back to the living room. "I've got some fresh Toomer's coffee. Want some? And I smell chocolate chip cookies."

"Sure." Lauri followed her through the living room to the kitchen. "The cookies are still warm."

Kade brought up the rear, and he went to put fresh water in Samson's bowl. The dog nudged his hand, then began to drink. Zorro joined him. The kitchen was a bit of a mess with flour and sugar all over the wood floor and the new granite tile counter.

Lauri glanced around. "You've redecorated. I like the birdhouses. Those ceramic chickens at Martha's house freak me out. They are *everywhere*." She shuddered. "Even in the kitchen wallpaper."

Bree measured beans into the coffee grinder while Kade got down mugs. The rich smell of the beans filled his nose.

"Naomi told her mother it was time for a new look," Bree said. "Martha loves those chickens, though." She pointed to the cookie plate. "Want to put those on the table? And there are peanut butter ones in the cookie jar."

Lauri carried the plate and the jar to the table. "So, big brother, what new sin have I committed now? I could tell I'm in trouble by the way you said my name."

Kade glanced at Bree, then back to Lauri. "Why didn't you tell me that you'd moved?"

Lauri's careful smile vanished. She opened the lid to the cookie jar and extracted a cookie before she spoke. "I didn't think it mattered. When you come to see me, we usually meet at the coffee shop. It's not a big deal."

"What do you know about Frannie Hastings?"

Lauri's eyes widened, and she put down the cookie. "Where did you hear that name and how did you know I moved?"

Kade kept his tone neutral. "We talked to Garrick's roommate. He mentioned that though he didn't know Garrick well, the next-door neighbor did. And he gave us the name of that neighbor. You."

Lauri slumped back in her chair. "Great."

"So what's this all about, Lauri?" Kade asked.

Lauri bit her lips. "I've done some dumb things in my life. If you think I haven't noticed, you'd be wrong. I wanted to do something to make you proud of me."

"But what does that have to do with Garrick and the missing girl? And I *am* proud of you, Lauri. Your grades have been great."

It was small praise and he knew it, but it was the best he could come up with on short notice.

Lauri made a face. "I want to be like Bree." Her gaze went to her sister-in-law. "I found out something about Garrick. Something that made me think he might have had something to do with Frannie Hasting's disappearance."

Bree poured cream into the coffee, then carried the mugs to the table. She handed a cup to each of them. "Did you talk to the sheriff?"

Lauri's fingers curled around the mug. "Garrick was

acting funny after she went missing. And he told Frannie he'd figured out a way to make enough money to finish his degree. She was curious about it, and he promised to tell her on their weekend away."

"That hardly sounds sinister," Bree said. "She appears to have fallen through the ice."

"But Samson didn't react, right?"

Bree frowned. "No, but he found her things. I did take him out on the ice, but he didn't seem to smell anything."

"Something about the whole thing seemed off to me. When she went missing, I moved into the apartment next door. When Garrick and Andy were both gone one day, I got into Garrick's room."

"You broke in?" Kade asked, not bothering to hide his disapproval.

Lauri hunched defensively. "The door wasn't locked."

Kade sighed. "What did you find?"

"Her necklace. And she *never* took it off. If she'd fallen through the ice, it wouldn't have been in his room."

"Maybe it fell off in his room," Bree said. "You can't jump to conclusions, Lauri."

"I know. So I went through his cell phone. I found a text where Garrick had asked her to go camping with him two days before she disappeared. The date was set for the day she went missing."

Bree gasped and sat down. "Did you talk to the police about this?"

Lauri hung her head. "I didn't have any proof. But I could tell Garrick liked me so I played along. I was supposed to pick him up after the drop and we would head for a cabin on the north side of Little Piney Lake. I hoped to find out something about Frannie."

"So that's why you were there." Kade's gut clenched. "Lauri, the duct tape? It was in his backpack."

Lauri pumped her fist in the air. "I *knew* it!" She looked thoughtful. "I wonder if he realized I was on to him."

Bree put her coffee on the table and leaned forward. "You put yourself in extreme danger. He could have hurt you or worse. You should have come to me and Kade."

Lauri looked mutinous. "I can take care of myself. I had Mace in my bag."

Kade glanced at Bree. "We have to get Mason in on this."

Bree's gaze was faraway. "Do you think you could find the cabin? I'd love to bring closure to Frannie's parents. I talked to them after the search. Such a nice family."

Lauri bolted upright. "I don't know exactly where it is, but I have one of her sweaters in a bag in my room.

I wanted to try to see if Samson could find where she'd been."

Kade leaped to his feet. "Let's go."

~இஉ⌐

Bree went to grab her search-and-rescue backpack out of the entry closet. Samson began running around and barking when she got out his search vest. He was so excited he kept sliding on the polished wood floors. She slipped the vest on him. He was always eager to work.

Kade took out his cell phone. "I'll see if Naomi will keep Dave."

Bree pulled her snow gear from the closet. "Davy will be disappointed if you don't fly the airplane with him. Lauri and I can handle this, right, Lauri?"

Kade frowned. "I'd like to come along in case there's trouble."

She tried to signal her concern to him in her gaze. "What kind of trouble could there be? Even if he was some kind of criminal, Garrick is dead. We're just going to see if we can find his lair, maybe find Frannie's remains." Bree had met the worried parents a month ago. She still had their phone number, and she'd love to be able to give them some closure. "We'll be back as quickly as we can."

Kade still frowned. "What about calling Naomi? You need a partner."

"I'm her partner and I've got Zorro," Lauri said. "He's not as well trained in search-and-rescue as Samson, but we'll be a team. Please, I want to do this."

Kade took a deep breath, then released a slow exhale. "Okay. The two of you are perfectly competent." Kade pressed his lips together, then kissed Bree. "Okay. I'll take care of Dave. Call me the minute you hear something."

Lauri stood on tiptoe and brushed her lips across his cheek. "Thanks, big brother." She called her dog over to her. "Got an extra search vest? I didn't bring his with me."

"Sure do." Bree rummaged in the closet and pulled out a bright orange vest.

Lauri slipped it on, and Zorro nearly preened. "Let's go." She yanked on her coat and rushed through the door.

Kade still looked worried, so Bree hugged him. "You wanted her to grow up, Kade. I'm proud of her. She went on the hunt for a good cause. I know sometimes it seems she's all about what *she* wants, but this time she just wanted to help. Something has changed her."

"I know you're right." He hugged her, then released her. "Be careful out there. The temperature has come up some, and you might get buried by snow sliding off tree branches."

"We'll be fine. We have Samson." Her dog whined

at the mention of his name, then went to the door and stood waiting. She smiled and put her hand on the door-knob. "My prince is calling."

"Here, I thought I was your only prince."

"No, you're the king." She blew him a kiss, then joined Lauri, who was tying her boots, on the porch.

The sun shone today, glinting on the snow and ice. Bree sat in a cold chair and laced her snow boots. "What drove you to do this, Lauri?"

Lauri tucked her long brown hair into her knit cap, then tugged the fabric over her ears. "Just what I said. I've watched you and Kade, you know. It might look like I chaffed against the restrictions—and I did—but I still noticed what you did and said. The more I've seen, the more I've wanted to be a person like you, Bree. One who cares about other people and puts others first."

Bree straightened. "I think there's more to it than that. Though it's very flattering, something special must have triggered you to get involved in this mystery."

Lauri pulled on bright-blue gloves. "I was home at Thanksgiving, and we were sitting around the fireplace playing Scrabble. It seemed such a mundane thing to be doing. I mean, come on, Scrabble is an old person's game. It's been around forever. You plopped the word *OTHERS* onto the board. In that moment, I realized my entire life was about me. I never thought of others at all.

It was always what *I* wanted. Because my parents died, I thought I was entitled to get whatever else I needed. I'd been searching for love and acceptance in all the wrong places when all the time it was right here."

Bree studied Lauri's face and saw her eyes mist. "Oh, honey, we love you so much. Kade would walk on hot coals for you."

"I know he would." Lauri's voice was choked. "I've put you both through a lot, and I'm sorry. Truly." She wiped her wet face with a finger. "I need to apologize to Kade too."

"I could see he was touched that you were trying to help that girl." Bree rose when Lauri did and grasped her shoulders. "But don't you dare put yourself in jeopardy like that again. That guy might have hurt you. Or worse."

Lauri sobered. "I know it was stupid. I need to be smart—like you."

Bree shook her head and smiled. "I'm stupid myself on occasion." She turned toward the Jeep. "Let's find that cabin."

SEVEN

M-18 HEADED ON EAST, AND BREE MADE A SHARP TURN
onto Pakkala Road, which would take them into a heav-
ily forested area. In the spring, motor homes and SUVs
pulling campers plied the road on their way to experience some of the last wilderness left in the Midwest.
Today the road was practically empty, as most campers
didn't want to enter the Snow King's paradise.

Some would laugh at her for describing snow country
as paradise, but then they likely had never smelled the
cold freshness of pollution-free air or watched a white
blanket of snow cloak everything in clean, pristine beauty.
Bree couldn't imagine a better place on earth. A sparkling
winter day like this offered a glimpse of perfection.

She parked the Jeep and got the dogs out. "Hang on
to Zorro."

Lauri nodded and yanked on her struggling dog's collar. "He wants to play in the snow."

"Little Piney Lake is that way." Bree gestured to the west. "You said it was on the north side of the lake. We'll have to hike in about two miles, then head toward the lake. I think we're just north of the lake if we head west."

Lauri's warm breath fogged the winter air. "Two miles? We can't get any closer?"

Bree shook her head. "I only have one sidecar for the snowmobile, so our only option is to hike in. It's not a bad walk, though. The ground is mostly level. Follow me."

She held a downed barbed-wire fence out of the way for Lauri, then the two of them trudged through the forest. The cold air burned Bree's lungs, so she knew Lauri had to be uncomfortable, but the young woman made no complaints. She pushed on with a grim and determined expression.

Half an hour later Bree paused. "We're close enough to let the dogs try to find the scent." She held the paper sack under Samson's nose. He plunged his nose into the jacket, then raised his muzzle and barked.

"Search, Samson," Bree said. Her dog raced off into the clearing.

Lauri unclipped Zorro's leash, and he ran after Samson. Both dogs ran back and forth, their muzzles in the air. They worked in a Z pattern, scenting the air until they could catch a hint of the one scent they sought—skin rafts drifting in the air. Samson's tail stiffened, and he turned and raced in the direction of the frozen lake.

"He's caught it!" Bree ran after her dog.

Lauri followed Zorro. The forest engulfed them again, and the rustling of the wind through the snow-covered trees, the muffled sounds of small animals, and the whispering scent of wet snow all comforted Bree with a sense of place and time. In spite of their familiarity, Bree knew the welcome was just a facade. The North Woods was never safe.

As Garrick Harper had found out.

The dogs leaped over snow-covered logs and darted around small bushes and stands of pine. The tree canopy dimmed the sun here, and Bree squinted to see through the shadows. Was that a cabin ahead? She pointed and Lauri nodded. The dogs reached the cabin and stood barking at the door.

Bree stopped at the front of the structure and peered inside. The windows were too dirty and the light was too dim to make out much more than the shadowy outlines of some rough furniture. Samson barked and ran in circles around her. "She's here somewhere. He's too excited."

She tried the door. Locked. Samson lunged at her and grabbed her coat sleeve in his teeth, then pulled her toward the corner of the house. "He wants me to go with him. Let's see if there's a back door. Search, Samson. Show me."

Her dog barked and raced to the back of the cabin where he leaped against the door. This door was locked as well. They would have to break in, something she hated to do. What if Garrick hadn't owned this place?

Samson flung himself against the door again. "Easy, boy. We'll get in there." She dropped her backpack from her shoulder and dug out the satellite phone, but there wasn't a good signal here. Too many trees. She'd have to find a clearing to call Mason and ask for permission to break the door.

"Bree?" Lauri's voice sounded panicked. She came around the corner of the building. "I think someone's in there. I heard something."

The owner? Bree pressed her ear against the door. Sure enough, there was a muffled thump from inside. "It might be an animal." She rapped on the door. "Hello? Anyone in there?"

At the sound of her voice, a frenzied pounding began as though a chair was being thumped on the floor. Samson began another volley of frenzied barking. He leaped at the window and smashed through the glass. His tail was wagging as he disappeared through the opening.

"I'm going in." Leaving her backpack where it lay on

the back porch, Bree rushed to the window. "Give me a leg up. I'll unlock the door when I get inside."

She fitted her boot into Lauri's cupped hands, then went headfirst through the window. A rough cabinet was under the window, so she grasped the edge of the wood and pulled herself all the way through until she crouched on top of the cabinet.

Samson was barking in the living room. Bree hopped down and ran to the door. She struggled with the rusty lock and finally got the door open. "Follow me!" Zorro raced past her feet. Her heart burned in her chest as she wheeled and ran after him.

She burst through the doorway into the living room. Her gaze swept the room and took in the rounded log walls, the smeared windows, the battered floors. There was a chair in one corner with a leg missing and a sofa with its back facing her. A wooden table held only a small key that wouldn't fit the door. A stepladder perched in another corner.

"Hello?"

Samson barked at a grungy brown sofa, and his ruff stood at attention. He tried to get his head under the couch but didn't succeed. Zorro joined him, and both dogs were clearly excited.

She glanced around. What was it she'd heard earlier? "Hello? Anyone in here?"

Something under her boots thumped and a voice called out. She and Lauri stared at one another, then Lauri shoved the sofa out of the way to reveal a door in the floorboards. A shiny padlock kept the door in place.

"The key!" Bree grabbed the small key from the table and fitted it into the lock. When it sprang open, she removed it and yanked on the door.

Lauri had her flashlight out, and she shone it into the darkness yawning in the hole below. The yellow glow illuminated the face of a young blond woman. Bree recognized her immediately. "Frannie?"

The young woman burst into tears. "Get me out of here, please get me out of here, Lauri!"

There were no stairs to the basement area. Bree looked around for a rope or something to help haul Frannie out.

"The ladder." Lauri bolted to get it.

She lowered it into the dark hole, and Frannie scrambled up it, then fell sobbing at their feet. Lauri sprang to her side and put her arm around Frannie.

Shivering, Frannie clasped herself and rocked back and forth. "I thought I was going to die in there."

"You're Frannie Hastings." Bree uncapped a bottle of water and offered it to the young woman.

Frannie took several gulps. "Thanks. I-I didn't think anyone would ever find me."

"How'd you get locked in there?" Bree asked.

"Garrick." Frannie shuddered. "I—I found out what he was doing."

"He locked you in there?" Lauri sounded outraged.

Frannie nodded. "I shouldn't have told him I was going to tell the Department of Natural Resources. I was just so shocked—you know? And I love wolves."

"Wolves?" Bree touched Frannie's head and found it cool. "You're not feverish." She helped her to a chair. "Can you tell us what happened?"

Frannie's hand trembled as she lowered the bottle from her mouth. "I thought he was going to tell me he was selling drugs or something. I could have lived with that. But he was bringing in people to kill wolves! I couldn't abide that. We've just gotten them repopulated up here."

Lauri's eyes were wide. "That's how he was making the money to stay in school?"

Frannie nodded. "It's disgusting. I started to cry and told him I was going to turn him in."

Kade would be upset when he heard this too. Bree put her hand on Frannie's shoulder. "He left you food and water? You seem in pretty good shape."

Frannie's tears came again. "When he didn't come back, I started conserving the food and water he'd left. I drank the last of the water this morning." She swigged the bottle of water again. "If I'd died, it would have ruined everything. I get to meet my birth mom for Christmas this year."

"You're adopted?" Lauri's voice trembled.

Frannie nodded. "I talked to my birth mom on the phone a few days before Garrick and I came here. I have a half brother I've never met too. They would have thought I ran away because I didn't want to meet them or something." Her voice broke and she stood. "Did someone call the cops? We have to get out of here before Garrick comes back."

"Garrick's dead, honey." Bree squeezed the young woman's shoulder. "Let's get you checked out and call your parents. Both sets." Only then did she see the trail of blood on the floorboards and the way her dog wasn't putting weight on his front left leg. "Samson's been hurt!"

After dropping Davy off with Naomi, Kade had joined his wife and sister in the waiting room. The squeak of the nurses' shoes in the halls mingled with the murmur of low-pitched voices in the Rock Harbor General Hospital as he entered the waiting room holding two cups of coffee. They sat in a row of chairs along the west wall with their dogs at their feet, still in their search vests. The scent of antiseptic was strong.

He touched Samson's head when the dog rose to greet him. "He's got a bandage. What happened?" He handed the coffee to Bree and Lauri, then sat in the gray upholstered chair next to his wife.

Bree took a sip. "Thanks, honey." She snapped her fingers to call the dog. "He cut his muzzle leaping through the window to show us where Frannie was. The vet met us here and put in a few stitches. The worst thing is he broke his leg too. It's in a splint right now, but he'll have to have it cast."

"He's always the hero." Kade leaned over and patted the dog, making sure not to touch his injury. "Frannie's parents are on their way?"

Bree's eyes filled. "I cried with them. I know what it's like to receive a child back from the dead. They should be here in the next half hour. Her birth mom is coming too. They'll be able to all meet before Christmas."

He well remembered the day they'd found Davy, missing for a year after Bree's first husband's plane went down in the North Woods. "How's Frannie doing? Do we know what happened?"

"She found out Garrick was helping others poach wolves. He had found a pack. She freaked out and was going to turn him in. He panicked, I think, and threw her in the basement."

Poor girl. Kade shuddered at all she'd gone through. "So why lock her in that basement?"

Lauri straightened. "I think he didn't know what to do with her. Frannie said he locked her up and told her he had to think about what to do next."

His baby sister had actually grown up. Kade wanted to hug her. "So where did you fit into this? I still can't believe you figured all this out on your own, Lauri."

She smiled and glanced at Bree. "I had a good teacher." Her expression turned solemn. "I thought he'd killed Frannie. I made friends with him and tried to figure out what he'd done with her. I think somehow he figured out I was on to him and planned to throw me in the cellar with her." She shuddered.

"And then what?" Kade asked. "He kept her there for two weeks!"

"I think he was in over his head and was getting ready to flee the country for Canada. He kept taking boxes into his house."

"He would have left you both trapped there?" Kade curled his hands into fists.

Lauri sobered. "I think so, Kade. He hadn't been back to see her in a week. She was out of food and water when we got there. No one would have been the wiser."

Kade's eyes burned, and he gulped back the lump in his throat. "I couldn't bear to lose you, Lauri." He jumped up and paced the waiting room, ignoring the surprised expressions of a family huddled in another corner. "I thought you were safe."

Lauri put her coffee on the table next to her and got up from her chair. She touched Kade's arm. "I'm beginning to realize that safety is an illusion. One thing I've learned from you and Bree is that every day is a gift. What we do with it is our choice. For too many years I've been throwing my days away on frivolous things, things I thought would make me happy. But they didn't. Finding Frannie—*that* made me more than happy. Satisfied, content, joyous. I had a purpose."

Her blue eyes were calm and at peace. Had he ever seen her so contented? If so, it was a long time ago, well before their parents died. Drawing her into his arms, he rested his chin on her head. Lauri wasn't a little girl anymore. She was growing into a strong woman.

"I love you, little sis," he whispered into her hair.

She let her cheek rest on his chest. "Love you too, big brother." After a moment, she pulled away. "And Frannie made me realize I was wrong about Zoe. I was thinking about myself and not her. I'm going to let Hilary and Mason tell her the truth."

"I'm glad," he whispered.

A couple burst through the hospital doors. The pale woman was blond and appeared to barely be holding it together. She wore designer jeans and supple leather boots.

The man, tall with salt-and-pepper hair, supported her as they rushed down the hall toward the waiting room.

The woman's eyes widened when she saw Bree with Samson by her feet. "Are you Bree Matthews?"

Bree rose and nodded. "Your daughter is going to be fine. The doctor was just out here. They'll let you see her shortly. She's just suffering from exposure and dehydration. They're giving her fluids."

Mrs. Hastings sagged and Bree caught her. "Thank God, thank God," the woman gasped. Tears pooled in her eyes. "I can't believe she's alive. Alive! I can't begin to thank you."

Bree reached over and grabbed Lauri's arm. "This is who found your daughter, Mrs. Hastings. She worked tirelessly to find out what had happened."

The woman grabbed Lauri and hugged her tightly. "Thank you." Her voice was a choked whisper. "You brought my little girl home."

Over Mrs. Hastings's shoulder, Kade saw Lauri's eyes fill with tears. They'd all been changed by the experience, and Lauri most of all.

Eight

Light slanted through the window, glinting off the ice on Lake Superior. Bree rubbed her eyes, then sat up from where she'd fallen asleep on the sofa. What was wrong with her? Ever since they'd found Frannie two weeks ago, she'd been so tired. Cassie would be here tomorrow, and Bree had a million things to do.

A horn honked outside, and she glanced at her watch. Her doctor's appointment! Naomi was the one honking. Bree grabbed her coat and ran toward the door where she slipped her feet into her boots. "You can't go," she told Samson, who stared back at her reproachfully, his head on his cast. "Oh, all right. Come on. But you'll have to stay in the car."

The dog limped around her feet, then trotted outside ahead of her. He was already used to dealing with the cast. She slogged through the snow to Naomi's mini-van, let Samson into the back, then practically fell into the seat beside Naomi. "Sorry. I fell asleep." She buckled her seat belt.

Naomi studied Bree's face and frowned. "You look awful. If I didn't know better, I'd think Kade gave you two black eyes." Naomi slid the gear into Drive and drove onto the pavement. "I'm glad you're going to the doctor today. I'm worried about you."

Bree leaned her head against the seat rest and smiled. "You and Kade are just alike. Worrywarts."

Naomi shrugged. "Guilty as charged. Have you heard from Lauri?"

Bree couldn't stop the smile from curving her lips. "She called last night. Her last class is tomorrow, and she offered to pick Cassie up from the airport on her way down."

"Full house for Christmas. It will be fun." Naomi stopped in front of the doctor's office. "I think I'll take Samson to the park until you get back. Will you be okay or would you rather I went with you?"

Samson's ears perked at the word *park*. He pressed his nose against Bree's neck and woofed. "Yeah." She managed a small smile. "I think Samson's all for it. Thanks, Naomi. For always being there for me."

She squeezed her friend's hand, then got out and

jogged into the building. The doctor had set up office in one of the old Victorian storefronts right downtown. It had been completely renovated and smelled of new carpet. She'd barely sat down when the nurse called her back.

The nurse appeared to be about fifty with dark eyes and high cheekbones that betrayed her Ojibwa heritage. Her smile was warm. "Dr. Wilson thought we'd save time if we drew some blood and got a urine sample."

She directed Bree to the lab in the back of the building. Fifteen minutes later Bree made her way back to the front and was escorted to a waiting room. Though the doctor was the new GP in town, Bree had seen him several times and liked him well enough. He seemed quite competent. She perched on the paper-clad table in her paper dress and waited. The table wasn't comfortable, but at least she could rest a little. Her lids were as heavy as the fog over the lake. She could almost curl up here and take a nap.

The door opened, and Dr. Wilson stepped inside. In his midthirties, he always dressed in jeans and a flannel shirt with hiking boots. Not the typical doctor type. "Well, Bree, you look like something Samson dragged in from the yard." He smiled at his own joke. "When you called, you said you wondered if you might have mono. Those tests are clear. It's not mono." His smile widened. "It's something very different."

"Depression?" That was second on her list of suspects.

His eyes sparkled, and he put his hand on her shoulder. "Nope. According to your urine test, you're pregnant."

"What?" She leaped to her feet, then reached around to clutch the paper wrap to keep it from blowing up. "Wha-What did you say?"

"Pregnant, as in, you're going to have a baby."

"That's impossible." Her pulse throbbed against her ribs. Did she dare hope?

His brows raised, and his pale-blue eyes sparkled. "Hmm, well, I could explain the birds and the bees to you but I don't think that's quite what you meant." His grin widened. "I thought you'd be happy about this, Bree."

Her spirit welled up within her, even as her eyes burned. "You're sure? I-I don't want to get my hopes up. Or Kade's."

"I'm sure. In fact, let me have them run an HCG level on some of that blood. That will tell us a lot. Hang on a minute." He exited the room.

Bree gulped in air. She stood and paced. "Don't get your hopes up," she muttered to herself.

The door opened and the doctor stepped back inside. "I'll have those tests in a few minutes. In the meantime, let's do an exam."

Bree shut her eyes while he examined her. *Please, please, God.*

"Hmm," Dr. Wilson said. "I don't think we have to wait on those tests. You're definitely pregnant. I'd say about three months along. When was your last period?"

Her eyes flew open, and she stared into his smiling face. "September, but it was very light. No doubts?"

"Nope." He grabbed her hand and helped her sit up. "That explains your fatigue. Any morning sickness?"

"A little queasiness, but I . . . thought it was stress." She couldn't hold the smile back any longer. Or the tears. "I can't wait to tell Kade." The sobs building in her throat choked her. "Thank you so much, Doctor. When will we know if everything is going to be okay? If I'll keep this baby? I lost the last one so early, though. Surely being this far along is much better. I can't believe I didn't recognize the symptoms, but now that I know, it makes perfect sense."

"I think I'll put you on a bit of progesterone. It will help ensure things stay good. But if you've made it this far, I don't think you'll need it. It won't hurt, though." He looked up when another nurse, this one a young blonde, poked her head in and held out a paper. He took the test results and scanned them. "Your HCG levels are good and high. I'd say we can be quite optimistic."

She put her hands to her cheeks. "I can't believe it."

"I'd advise you to see your obstetrician in Houghton

since you lost the last baby. Just send me a birth announcement." He winked, then left the room.

Bree put her palms on her hot cheeks. A baby! She leaped from the table and twirled around the room.

"I'm going to have a baby!" she yelled to no one in particular.

⁓ℐℰℓ⁓

Kade frowned when he realized the lights were off in the house. Bree must still be at the doctor's, but her appointment had been hours ago. He wished she'd let him go along. She was more likely not to tell the doctor how bad she'd been feeling.

Samson met him at the door. Kade sniffed the aromas in the air as he stomped the snow from his feet, then rubbed Samson's head. "Smells like herring. Your mom hates herring." He kicked off his boots and followed the delicious scent.

His first impression of the house had been wrong. It wasn't dark. Candles flickered on the table and the fireplace mantel. "Bree?"

Wearing a dark-green dress and heels, she appeared in the doorway from the kitchen. Her red hair was in soft curls around her heart-shaped face, and her smile lit up the room with no need of the candles. The silver tray in her hand held what looked like a treat he hadn't had in ages.

He could barely tear his gaze away from his wife, but she held up the tray, obviously expecting a comment. "Is that *nakkikääröt*?" The sausage rolls were one of his favorites. "And I could swear I smell herring."

"Right on both counts." She came toward him and extended the tray. "They're still hot."

He picked one up. "Oh, ouch, you weren't kidding." He blew on it, then took a bite. The flavors hit his tongue and he nearly groaned. "Where's Dave?"

"At Naomi's." She was still smiling.

He gobbled the last of the food. "What did the doctor say? Has he given you some magic medicine to cure you?"

She put the tray on the table. "This is a condition we'll have to live with for a while."

He stilled. "Is it serious?" Fear grabbed him by the throat and wouldn't let go.

Her smile was playful. "It depends on what you mean by serious. It's going to disrupt our lives. Neither of us will likely get any sleep for months."

He studied her face. "Spill it, Green Eyes. What's wrong with you? It can't be too bad with that smile on your face."

She took his hand and guided it to her belly. "What do you want more than anything, Kade?"

He searched her clear green eyes, those eyes he loved so much. "You, Bree. Always you."

"Other than that. What would make our life complete?" Her gaze grew sober, and she pressed his hand harder against the soft mound of her belly.

He could have sworn his heart stopped in his chest, that he forgot to draw in air as her meaning sank in. "You don't mean . . . ," he whispered.

She nodded. "A baby, Kade. We're going to have a baby."

He whooped and lifted her in his arms. Samson barked and chased them as he whirled her around the room. Both of them laughing, laughing until the tears ran.

NINE

ALL WAS READY FOR THE EVENING FESTIVITIES AS BREE glanced around the room. The evergreen tree touched the high ceilings in the lighthouse living room, and hundreds of twinkling white lights lifted her mood to the sky. The strong scent of pine mingled with that of the pumpkin-spice candles flickering on the fireplace mantel.

The clock on the mantel sounded seven, and she looked out the window where the lamplight glimmered on the snow. No sign of them yet.

Kade finished connecting the iPod, and Christmas music began to spill from the speakers. "You're antsy." His grin told her he was too.

Davy was on the floor with his head on Samson's flank. Five-year-old Zoe had her head on Samson's other side. Anu, Bree's first husband's mother, was helping Hilary put the finishing touches on dinner. They'd insisted on cooking tonight. Mason had been called out on a car accident, but he was due to arrive shortly as well.

"Lauri texted me that Cassie had arrived," Davy said.

"When was that?" Bree asked.

"About an hour ago, I think." He came to a seated position. "Can we open a present tonight? Just one? It's only a day early."

A smile curved her lips. "Maybe."

He leaped to his feet and threw his arms around her waist. "Thanks, Mom!"

She debated giving him the present before the girls got in, then Samson lifted his head and jumped up. He padded toward the door.

"They're here," Kade said.

Her pulse jumped in her throat when she saw Cassie's familiar tangle of shoulder-length curls. Bree flung open the door and stepped into the cold wind when Cassie reached the porch.

Cassie returned Bree's exuberant embrace. "I've missed you!"

A lump lodged in Bree's throat, and she stepped back and stared at her sister. "You are blooming. Washington must agree with you. Come in. Samson will be disappointed you didn't bring his buddy Bubbles."

Cassie followed her inside. "I thought about it, but it's a long flight, and he was happy staying with my roommate." She sniffed the air, then smiled. "Anu's *pulla*?"

Bree linked arms with her sister. "Piles of it. All yeasty and warm right from the oven. And her pancakes for breakfast. She's promised to come over early."

"Is she here now?"

"She's in the kitchen with Hilary and the gang." Over her sister's shoulder, Bree saw Lauri's smile dim. "Zoe is in the living room."

Lauri straightened but her smile was more of a grimace. Bree knew Lauri would bolt if she could. Seeing the child she'd given up for adoption was always painful.

"Look who's here," Bree announced when they reached the living room.

Davy leaped to his feet and rushed to Cassie. His green eyes were flashing with excitement "Aunt Cassie, did you bring me a new airplane for Christmas?"

Bree put her hand on her son's head. "David Robert, you know better than to ask for gifts."

Cassie had started the boy's obsession with small airplanes two years ago at Christmas, and Bree suspected one of the boxes Kade was carrying in from the trunk held another of his favorites. She had to admit she was eager to see what else Cassie had brought. She thought of the most unusual gifts.

Davy ducked his head. "Sorry."

Cassie smiled and hugged him. "You'll know tomorrow."

Hilary appeared in the doorway. She wore her blond hair looser and softer now, in waves around her face. Her feet were bare, and her tender smile lingered on her daughter.

Her smiles came easily now, and one popped into place when she saw Cassie. It faltered only a little when she spied Lauri. "I thought you two had arrived. Mother is dying to see you both. We've got fresh coffee on. If you ask nicely, Mother might let you have some pulla before dinner."

Lauri's gaze lingered on Zoe.

When Zoe saw she had Lauri's attention, she twirled. "See my dress?" Red velvet swirled around her white tights.

"Very pretty, Zoe," Lauri said.

The little girl preened, then plopped beside Samson and threw her arms around his neck. He licked her cheek and she giggled.

Lauri followed Hilary to the kitchen. Bree went too with her arm locked in Cassie's. The news was nearly ready to burst out of her. She didn't know how she would be able to keep it in until they had dessert around the fireplace.

Bree waited as Kade poked at the fire in the hearth until it was blazing. She glanced at her watch. Eight thirty. The adults had squeezed onto the sofa and every available chair while the children lounged on the floor with Zorro and Samson. Elvis crooned "On a Snowy Christmas Night" in the background.

Bree's heart swelled at the words of the song. *"Give thanks for all you've been blessed with."* Her family was all here, the entire hodgepodge mix of Rob's family and Kade's, as well as her sister. They all made one whole. The group wouldn't be complete without one another. She wouldn't have changed a thing about her life in this one moment or these precious loved ones who brightened her life and accepted her for who she was.

Through a mist of tears, her gaze found Kade's. He looked a little teary-eyed himself, and she knew the words had impacted him as well.

Hilary rose. "I think we can let the children have one special package each. Lauri, do you want to give your present? Your Uncle Mason and I have one for you, Dave." She signaled to her husband who disappeared into the office, then reappeared with a huge grin and a red bicycle.

Davy whooped and ran to hug his aunt and uncle. "Cool! It's a ten-speed."

While he examined his new bike, Lauri rose and pulled a box from under the tree. Pink princess paper swathed it. She sat on the floor beside Zoe and handed it to the toddler.

Zoe's eyes were big. "A present!" She tore into the wrapping paper until the Cabbage Patch doll's face appeared. When she struggled with the package, Lauri helped her.

"Mama Lauri really wanted you to have it early," Hilary said in a matter-of-fact voice. "You grew in her tummy until you were big enough to go home with us to your special room. Thank her for your present."

The child stared at Lauri's belly, then smiled. "Thank you, Mama Lauri."

Bree's throat tightened at the expression on Lauri's face, then mouthed, "Thank you" at her sister-in-law. Hilary had been right about this.

She rose and grabbed the basket of small packages. "Kade and I have a special gift to give each of you. I want you to open them at the same time."

Kade stepped forward to help her pass around the small, gaily wrapped gifts. "Hang on, don't open them until we tell you." His voice trembled a little.

Bree could barely stand the suspense. "Here is yours, Anu." Kade handed out the other gifts.

Dressed in a creamy gown overlaid with exquisite

Finnish lace, Anu wore her fair hair high on her head in a coronet of braids and was always the lady. Anu's gift was a bib that read *I LOVE GRANDMA*. Bree couldn't wait for her to see it.

Anu held up the bib. "*Kulta*, is this true?"

"Our little one is due in July." Bree went to her knees in front of Anu. Though nearly sixty, Anu's shining hair held no trace of gray, and her face was as unlined as Bree's. From the moment Bree had married Rob and became a Nicholls, Anu had claimed her as one of her own, and Bree loved her so much.

Davy ripped his package open and lifted high a T-shirt that had *BIG BROTHER* on the back. "I'm getting a baby brother!" He leaped up and threw his arms around his mother, then raced to hug Kade.

"It might be a baby sister," Kade reminded him. "You already have Samson. He's your baby brother."

The dog's ears perked at the mention of his name. He pressed his head against Davy's knee.

"Samson's my *big* brother," Davy said. "He takes care of me. He takes care of everybody." He touched Samson's cast.

Cassie's and Lauri's gifts were teddy bears wearing diapers that read *BEST AUNT IN THE WORLD*. Hilary's gift was an *AUNT* coffee mug, and Mason's was wool hunting socks with a baby on each sole. As each of them ripped into their gifts, the shock and amazement brought more tears to Bree's eyes.

Cassie wiped her eyes. "How long have you known?"

"Just since yesterday." Bree's face hurt from smiling.

"You didn't let on." Lauri poked her brother. "I hope he has your good heart."

Kade's blue eyes smiled back. "I hope she has your courage."

She colored and dropped her gaze. "You're a good brother, Kade. So patient in spite of all I've put you through. I'm going to do better, I promise."

"I love you just the way you are, squirt." He hugged Lauri.

Watching them, Bree's tears overflowed. God was good, so good.

Epilogue

The nurse dimmed the lights and left them alone. Bree should be tired, but energy strummed along her veins and kept her lids wide-open. She stared into her husband's face as he drank in the baby's face in the crook of her arm.

Then switched his gaze to the baby in the other.

"Twins," he breathed. "I still can't believe it. The early ultrasound didn't show this."

Bree drew her finger along the downy face of her daughter. "The doctor said a twin hiding behind the other baby only happens in one percent of the cases. I guess God decided we needed a bonus." She raised her gaze to Kade's. "You have a son."

"And a daughter." He pressed a kiss on each downy head. "She's got your eyes and hairline."

"It's too soon to tell," she protested. But she saw it too. The tilt of their daughter's eyes, the tiny widow's peak along the hairline now hidden by the tiny cap. She inhaled the salty-sweet aroma a newborn carried for only a few weeks. "I want Davy. And Anu."

"And Naomi?"

"Of course." She wanted to show her children to the world. She watched Kade step to the door, but he didn't have to go far. Everyone was waiting right outside in the hall.

"Mommy!" Davy barreled into the room.

When was the last time he'd called her mommy? She patted the mattress. "You have a brother *and* a sister, honey."

"Both?" He stopped in his tracks, and his mouth formed an O. Then he gingerly clambered up beside Bree and stared at one baby, then the other. He reached out and his sister grasped his finger. "She likes me!" He beamed.

"Of course she does. You're her big brother. You have to protect her. Teach her all the things she doesn't know."

Behind him, Anu had stopped as well. Her tender gaze lingered on Bree's face, then moved to the infants in her arms. Tears sprang to her eyes and coursed down her cheeks. "Oh, kulta," she breathed. "God has blessed us with two."

"Come here, Grammy, and kiss those babies," Kade said. "They smell so good. They're still a little gooey, and they have sticky stuff in their eyes, but they're beautiful. And so's their mommy." His gaze locked with Bree's.

Naomi stepped into the room behind Anu. Her gaze took in both babies. "Girl, you never do anything halfway." She wiped her eyes and approached the bed behind Anu, who was pressing kisses against the pudgy cheeks of the tiny girl in her arms.

Anu laid Bree's daughter in Naomi's arms, then lifted the baby boy. "Do we have names?"

"We had a name for each, just in case." Neither of them had wanted to know the baby's sex. "Her name is Hannah, after you, Anu. Ann is the variation of Hannah. And our son is Hunter. For Samson."

Naomi rushed for the door. "I'm bringing Samson in. He needs to meet his new charges."

"They won't let you," Bree called. But she was talking to the wind. She and Kade exchanged rueful glances. She watched Anu settle into a chair with both babies in her arms. Davy hung over his siblings with rapt attention.

She heard the click of Samson's nails on the floor before she saw him. His broken leg had quickly healed and hadn't left a trace of a limp. With the dog on his leash and wearing his search vest, Naomi came rushing in, her cheeks pink and her eyes sparkling.

She released him from his leash. "I had to do some talking, but turns out Samson found the receptionist's grandson when he wandered off. Remember that, Bree? Samson is the star in this town. He gets special privileges."

Samson's dark, intelligent eyes went from Bree to the babies, who were still sleeping in Anu's arms. He whined, then went to sniff one baby then the other before turning to stare at Bree as if to say, *What have you done now?* Then he curled at the foot of her bed. His gaze dared anyone to hurt his family.

Kade eased onto the mattress beside Bree. He slipped his arm under her head, and she curled up next to him. Anu brought the babies to them, and they parted enough to settle the tiny forms between them.

"Me too!" Davy climbed onto the bed on Bree's other side.

She slipped her arm around him, then turned her gaze to lock with Kade's. The intensity in his eyes warmed her, made her forget the pain still slowing her movements.

"We have a full house," he whispered.

"And even fuller hearts," she said, leaning over to kiss him.

Reading Group Guide

1. Have you ever dealt with an ungrateful person? How did you deal with him or her?
2. Bree wanted a baby more than anything. Have you ever struggled with God saying, "Wait"? How did you handle it?
3. Kade was hard on his sister because he didn't want to fail his parents. What can make a parent cling too hard?
4. Lauri realized that every day is a gift. What do you think that means?
5. Lauri was looking for a purpose in life. Do you know what your purpose is?
6. How do you feel about adoption? Would you ever adopt a child of a different race or one with health problems?

7. Our families can often be a mishmash of members. Do you have an unusual member in your family?

8. Has God ever given you something over and above anything you've dreamed of?

DEAR READER,

WE ARE BACK IN ROCK HARBOR TOGETHER! IT HAS been so gratifying to see how much you have loved Bree and Samson. I love them too. And there's quite a lot of me in Bree, so it feels like your love extends to me personally.

I hope you enjoyed catching up with Bree and the gang. I smiled all the way through the ending myself!

As always, I love to hear from you! E-mail me anytime at colleen@colleencoble.com.

Your friend,
Colleen

HOLY NIGHT

ONE

THE FRESH AROMA OF THE SEA WAS WELCOME AFTER the stale air of the airplane. Leia Kahale inhaled, then swept her arm toward the broad expanse of the golden sand of Shipwreck Beach on Kaua'i's south shore. The waves were always treacherous here, but strong swells had been battering the island for three days and few people were in the water.

She pointed. "We could put the tent up here, Bane. I'd love for Makawehi Point to loom in the back for great wedding pictures. And with poinsettias, it will be just perfect."

Her fiancé, Bane Oana, draped his muscular arm around her shoulders. He wore black board shorts and a turquoise aloha shirt that looked good with his black hair. "Whatever you want, honey."

Leia lifted her face into the warm December breeze. Her heart felt full to bursting as she pressed against Bane's warm chest. "It seems almost wrong to be this happy."

Bane smiled down at her. "I haven't had any trouble adjusting to our new normal." He brushed a kiss across her lips. "I like your curves in that dress. I might have to fight off the other men on the beach."

The way her skin heated at his touch never failed to thrill her. How could one person affect her so dramatically? She held his face and kissed him again. "Do you know how much I've missed you?"

Bane's younger sister, Kaia, nudged him, breaking their kiss. She tucked her long dark hair behind her ears. "Hey, you two, we have work to do. Less kissing, more planning. The wedding is in five days. There are a ton of details to see to. Bane, I need you to run by The Beach House and pay for the rehearsal reception, then stop and pay the catering bill. Leia and I will show the staff where we want the tent and tables."

He groaned. "My fiancée just arrived from Moloka'i and I have to leave her to write checks?" He didn't drop his arm from around Leia.

"That would be a good guess." Kaia smiled and patted his arm.

Leia smiled and tipped her face up for another kiss.

His spicy scent made her heart speed up. Heat rushed to her cheeks at the realization they would only be apart a few more nights. "Talk to you tonight. Wait, when does Mano arrive?"

"About five. I'll pick him up, and we'll meet you at Kaia's for dinner." He lifted Leia in his arms. "Or maybe I'll just take you with me."

She laughed and kissed him again. "Put me down, you big oaf. We have work to do."

He sighed. "You know what they say about all work and no play. Look at that surf. It's just begging for a board."

"And we'll go surfing. But later." She smiled as he put her feet back on the ground. "And I'll fix you lomilomi salmon tonight to make it up to you."

His expression brightened. "I'll wax the board when I'm done. Don't be too late." He walked across the thick sand toward the Jeep parked in the lot across the street.

"Leia, look at this!" Her sister, Eva, waved to her from a tide pool. "There's a starfish." Her beautiful blond hair turned men's heads wherever she went until they noticed her Down syndrome features.

"In a minute, Eva." Leia ignored Eva's pout and turned back to face Kaia. "I love Bane so much, but I'm a little nervous. Will I be a good wife and mother? I mean, I didn't really have a great role model."

Kaia smiled and squeezed Leia's hand. "You know about giving to other people. You've practically raised Eva yourself, and look what a good job you've done with her. You and my brother are great together."

Leia sighed. "You're right. I know we are. It's just—"

A scream pierced the air behind them and a board shot up in the roiling waves off the beach. Then a hand waved.

Leia pointed out a dark head. "Someone's in trouble."

"Go get the lifeguard from the Hyatt!" someone yelled.

Kaia kicked off her OluKai slippers and ran for the heavy surf. Everyone on the beach gathered to watch as she plunged into the big waves and struck out toward the figure. She worked with dolphins and was an excellent swimmer, almost more at home in the water than on the land.

Leia joined the crowd and held her breath, praying all the while. Kaia reached the area where the hand had gone up, but the woman couldn't be seen. Kaia dove into the water, and seconds went by in an agonizing trickle until two heads popped up in the surf.

Only then did Leia exhale. She kicked off her slippers, then rushed to help Kaia bring the woman ashore. It would be a tricky exit from the sea here with the tide adding to the ocean's power. Kaia got close enough to stand, and she steadied the woman she'd just rescued, clearly a tourist from the beet-red sunburn on her face and arms.

Leia waded out a few feet, though it was all she could do to stand when the waves slammed into her. She licked her salty lips and watched for a break in the surf.

Kaia spoke to the woman, who nodded. Then, looking at the sea, Kaia grabbed her arm and propelled her toward the shore at the right time. As they neared, Leia took the woman's other arm and helped her as they staggered to the sand. The woman collapsed, and Kaia stood panting as a lifeguard rushed up.

The woman sobbed hysterically as the lifeguard checked her over. "I almost drowned." She looked up at Kaia. "Thank you, thank you."

"Glad I was able to help. You'll be all right."

Leia retreated a few more steps as a paramedic arrived. She glanced around for Eva. The tide pool where she'd been splashing was deserted. Leia moved toward the crowd. Eva might have been watching the rescue. But after two minutes Leia still hadn't caught sight of her sister's blond head.

Maybe she'd gone to get something to drink. Leia hurried to the Hyatt, but there was no one around the outdoor lagoon or the drink area. She retraced her steps to find Kaia standing by their abandoned shoes with a towel someone had given her. "Kaia, I can't find Eva."

Her friend frowned. "She has to be here somewhere."

"Maybe the excitement frightened her. She could be back at your car."

"Let's go check."

The women hurried past the Hyatt's main entrance to the parking lot. The little red Volkswagen Kaia drove was empty. Leia stopped a couple putting their things away in a van. "Have you seen a blond woman about twenty-three? She has Down syndrome and she was wearing a red sundress."

The woman, about forty with pudgy legs sticking out of her shorts, nodded. "I did just see her. She was with a man."

Leia's gut clenched. "Where did they go?" Eva trusted everyone, and Leia had to watch carefully to make sure men didn't take advantage of her.

The woman pointed. "Up the cliff."

Makawehi Cliff was a popular place with the locals to jump into the water, though it was dangerous, especially on a day like today. Eva would never do that on her own, even on a calm day.

Kaia started that way. "I'll check there, *mahalo*. Leia, you stay here in case she's just in the restroom or something. She'll panic if she can't find you." Kaia started across the parking lot toward the cliff.

"Hope you find her." The woman got in the van with her husband.

Dread congealed in Leia's stomach as she looked around the lot. A scrap of paper on the wipers caught her eye, and she stepped to the Volkswagen and retrieved it. She unfolded the note. The words jumped out at her and nearly drove her to her knees.

I have Eva. If you call the police, you'll find her dead body. If you tell Kaia or Bane, you'll find her body. Wait.

The paid catering bill was tucked in the pocket of Bane's board shorts when he walked into Tomkats. He smiled as his favorite cat sidled up and wound around his legs.

The scent of macadamia-encrusted mahimahi filled the space. A few locals and several tourists glanced up when he walked in, then went back to their meals. The tables were decorated for Christmas, and potted poinsettias added color to the plants growing in the courtyard.

He glanced around for his younger brother. He'd dropped Mano here while he stopped by the caterer's. Mano beckoned to him from a table in the back by the window. Broad and capable, Mano looked every inch a former Navy SEAL. He lifted his soft drink in Bane's direction. "You seem calm for a man about to be married. I thought Annie would have a nervous breakdown before our wedding. The craziness hasn't hit yet?"

Bane pulled out a chair and sat. "Leia is pretty calm about it all. We both are." He eyed his brother. "You've got that flat mouth. What's going on?"

Whenever Mano was dealing with something unpleasant, he pressed his lips together and didn't look Bane in the face. Mano ducked his head.

"Mano? Everything okay with Annie?"

His brother's head came up then. "Oh sure, Annie is great." He heaved a sigh. "I guess you have to know. They released Zimmer."

Bane straightened. "When?"

"Last week."

"And they're just now telling us?" Bane flopped back in his chair. "Don't they realize he's dangerous? Why didn't I get a call?"

"The DA called the house when they couldn't get you on your cell. You were probably diving. I took the call."

Bane was an oceanographer and did sea salvage. He was often where his cell phone didn't work. Dennis Zimmer, a name he'd tried not to think about the past few years. He and Zimmer had been friends once, but Bane had caught the ex–Coast Guard ensign stealing supplies and selling them. A Coast Guard seaman had been killed in the last heist. Bane had found the evidence and had been forced to testify against Zimmer, who was convicted of robbery and manslaughter.

He exhaled. "Is he headed this way?"

"The DA suspected he might be. When did you get the last letter from him?"

Bane thought back. "About a year ago, I think. I need to warn Leia to be careful." He rose. "I'd better go talk to the police and see if they can keep an eye on flights into Kaua'i."

"You haven't even eaten."

"I'm suddenly not very hungry." Bane strode out the door toward where he'd parked his Jeep.

He yanked open the door and slid inside. When he slammed the door, he realized the truck was tilted to the left like it was on something. He got back out and glanced at the tires on the right. They looked fine so he went around to the other side. Two tires rested on their rims. Closer inspection showed they'd been slashed.

The blood rushed from his head. Zimmer was already here.

Two

W*ait*. B*ut* L*eia* *couldn't just wait here for some*
unknown person to call her, not when she felt like she'd
just downed fifteen cups of coffee. And what was taking
Kaia so long to climb the cliff and get back?

Leia stared at the note. How could this kidnapper
even ask her to keep it from the man she loved? She
couldn't handle this without Bane.

Maybe it was someone trying to scare her. She eyed
the Hyatt. Eva could be in there chatting away with
someone. Or she could have spotted a monk seal down
the beach and gone to see it. She prayed this was a hoax
of some kind, someone's idea of a weird joke.

Slinging her bright orange beach bag over her
shoulder, she started back to the beach. Her cell phone
chirped in her bag, and she dropped to her knees and

dug for it. Her heart pounded as it rang four times, then five, before her fingers closed around it.

"Hello?" Her voice was breathless. "Eva?"

"Eva is fine. For now." The distorted voice on the other end had to be from a machine. "But if you don't do exactly as I say, you'll find her body under the Point. Dead."

"Don't hurt her." Leia licked her dry lips. "She's like a child."

"Then you'll do what I say. Go find lover boy and tell him you've got cold feet. You don't want to marry him after all."

Leia gripped the phone with a damp hand. "What? Why?"

"When you've done what I say and the wedding date is past, I'll release your sister."

"B-But that's five days away!" Leia's voice shook. "She'll be terrified. You have to let her go. Please, I'll do anything!"

"Then do what I tell you. And no police. Tell no one you've received this call. If you simply change the wedding date, I'll know. Make Bane believe you or Eva will be dead."

"You're asking me to do the impossible," she whispered. "Everyone will want to know where Eva is. Kaia is looking for her right now."

"When Kaia gets back, tell her you got a call from Eva asking if she could stay with a friend for a few days."

"No one will believe that!"

There was a pause. "Then come up with a story they *will* believe. Your sister's life is resting on you."

"Please, just let Eva go." Her eyes burning with the effort to hold back her tears, Leia paced the lot.

The call ended and she stared at her phone. This could not be happening. She scrolled through the received calls, but the last call was from a blocked number. No way to call him back.

Her knees went weak and she sank to the pavement. The hot concrete burned into her flesh, but even that pain didn't come close to the agony squeezing her lungs. The man had put her in an impossible position. She saw no way of convincing anyone that Eva was fine. And Bane would never believe she didn't want to marry him.

Yes, he will.

She'd dragged her feet long enough, making excuses for putting off the wedding. First it had been she couldn't desert her grandmother as she was making plans to move into an assisted-living place. Then she had to sell her *kapa* business, and that had taken awhile. The base of all of it was fear, plain and simple.

She'd buried herself in her little town on Moloka'i, happy to be in her element with people she knew. But as Bane's wife, they'd be traveling, meeting new people. Bane had been patient with her, but if she told him she'd changed her mind, he would think she didn't love him. Their past would be enough to convince him. She'd sent him away once before.

Her thoughts scattered like pikake petals in a hurricane. She had to convince the man she loved that she didn't want to marry him. How could she hurt him like that? But she had to do it to save Eva.

Kaia waved at her from the base of the cliff. Her face was pink from exertion, and her dark eyes were strained as she came toward Leia. "Eva jumped off the cliff with a man, but I can't find her."

Leia gasped, and spots danced in front of her eyes. How was that possible? She'd just talked to him. Could there be more than one person involved? "D-Did anyone see her after that?"

Kaia shook her head. "Let's look along the beach. Most people jump off that thing with no trouble."

Leia swallowed hard and squared her shoulders. "She knows better than to do that."

Kaia nodded and put her hand on Leia's arm. "If we can't find her, we have to call the Coast Guard. You know that."

"I-I know. But she'll be all right. I know she's all right."

"Of course she is." But Kaia's glance slid away. "Let's go look."

Tears finally escaped Leia's eyes. "Pray, Kaia."

Kaia took her hand. "I haven't stopped."

The sun was setting over the ocean to the west, bouncing rays of gold and pink off the water. Bane's stomach burned sourly. They'd walked two miles, all the way to Maha'ulepu Beach, a remote stretch of sand frequented only by locals. Still no sign of Eva. A Coast Guard cutter cruised offshore as well. Kaia and her husband, Jesse, were on another boat with Kaia's bottle-nosed dolphin, Nani. If Eva was out there, Nani would find her.

Eva could have been washed out to sea.

Or drowned.

He stepped closer to Leia, who stood on a rock at the edge of the water. She barely took her attention off the whitecaps rolling toward the golden sand. "We'll find her, honey." He put more confidence into his voice than he felt.

Tears shimmered in her eyes when she glanced at him before turning her attention back to the water. "I should have been watching her, Bane."

"There was a near drowning, Leia. Of course you

and Kaia wanted to help." A wave soaked his feet as he waded in closer to her and slipped his arm around her waist. "We're not doing her any good here. Let's go back to Shipwreck Beach and head the other direction."

"Mano and Annie went that way. They'll call if they find her." She glanced at him again. "Any word from Kaia?"

"She called a few minutes ago. Nani hasn't found anything."

She sagged against him, then turned and buried her face in his chest. He held her close without saying a word. What was there to say? They'd lived in the islands all their lives. No one knew the dangers of the sea better than the two of them. The muscles in her back were rigid and unyielding as if she was holding herself apart from him.

He stroked his hand along her spine and wished he could comfort her somehow. He still needed to tell her about Zimmer too. For all he knew, the man could be despicable enough to seek revenge by hurting Leia.

She pulled away and wiped her eyes. The sun sank faster now, plunging into the water like a fireball. "We'll ride back with Kaia and Jesse on the boat. It will be too dark to see the potholes in the lane. Look, they're coming in now for us."

She nodded and let him lead her into the water as the roar of Jesse's boat grew nearer. Nani swam up to them, chirping her friendly hello, and Bane rubbed her warm, rubbery body before helping Leia climb the ladder to the boat. He clambered aboard himself and moved to drop into a seat by his sister.

How's Leia? Kaia mouthed.

He winced and shook his head. His gaze found Leia where she sat with her head down. When she was like that, it was tough to get through the remoteness she'd pulled around her. She barely looked up when he moved to sit by her.

He took her hand, so cold and motionless. "Honey, talk to me. We have to hold to each other through this."

Her eyes were wide and unblinking. "This is my fault."

"You're just upset."

"No, I need to do a better job with Eva. If I hadn't been distracted . . . I don't think I can marry you, Bane. Eva needs me too much."

"Of course you can marry me. We'll find Eva and things will be back to normal soon. You'll see. Eva loves me. She wouldn't want to go back to life without me there. You know that as well as I do."

"I don't know." Leia exhaled with a rush of air, then turned her head and looked out over the dark sea. The tight line of her pressed lips broke his heart.

"Maybe she came ashore somewhere. She might be

wandering around lost. Her picture will be on the news tonight and in the paper. Someone will see her."

She shook her head. "I realize now this marriage is not the right thing for any of us." She pulled her hand away, then wrenched off her ring and handed it to him. "I'm not going to marry you, Bane. I'm sorry." The last word ended on a sob.

His fingers closed around the ring she pressed into his hand. He stared into her face. What was she thinking? This wasn't happening. She loved him. But staring into her remote eyes, he saw no spark of the constant love he was used to seeing.

He put the ring in his pocket. "We'll talk about it after we find Eva. You're just upset, and I don't blame you."

"I blame me," she whispered. "I should have known better."

Was she punishing herself—and him—for Eva's disappearance? He slipped his arm around her and tipped her face up to his. His lips found hers and his pulse sped at the way she kissed him back.

Then she jerked away. "Just because we have passion between us doesn't mean we belong together."

If that was how she felt, he didn't know her anymore. He gave her a long look, then moved to his side of the bench.

THREE

THE CLOCK ON THE BED STAND SHOWED 12:02, BUT A rooster still crowed in the dark beyond her window. A breeze blew in the scent of ginger from the flower bed outside. Leia lay on the guest bed at Kaia's with her eyes wide open. How could she sleep with Eva in such danger? And she kept replaying the hurt in Bane's eyes. She moaned and threw her hand over her eyes.

Her life had seemed so perfect. How could everything fall apart so quickly? She had to find Eva and get her back safely.

She sat up and swung her legs to the floor. Maybe some chamomile tea would help her sleep. She padded across the wood floor to the door. She put her hand on the doorknob, but her cell phone rang, a blaring sound in the still of the night. She leaped for the nightstand and snatched it up, sparing a glance at the display.

Blocked.

Her throat tightened. It was him. "Hello?"

"You haven't called off the wedding."

The electronically altered voice gave her chills. She tightened her grip on the phone. "I did! I gave him back his ring."

"The food has not been canceled."

She sank onto the edge of the bed. "They were closed by the time we finished searching for Eva."

He said nothing for a long minute. "If the food isn't canceled by noon, look for Eva's body."

A mental image came of Eva's long blond hair floating around her lifeless body. Leia choked back a wave of nausea. "I'll do it when they open at nine. Please. Don't hurt her."

"I don't like it when someone plays games with me."

She bit her lip. "I'm not playing games. I told you—there was a search going on for Eva, and I couldn't do anything about the food. They believed she might have drowned, and it was easier to let them think that rather than she'd gone off with a friend."

"I'll give you one more chance. Don't screw this up."

When the call dropped, she lowered her hand and stared at her phone. Could there be a way to trace him? She tossed her phone onto the bed. He'd said not to tell the police, but she was so ill equipped to find Eva by herself. Could she even trust him to follow through on his promise to release her sister? What if she did everything exactly as he said, but he killed Eva anyway? Leia would never be able to live with the regret.

She moaned and put her head in her hands. What should she do? No matter what she decided, it could all go horribly wrong.

She lifted her head at a soft knock on the door. "Yes?"

"It's me." Bane's deep voice spoke on the other side of the door.

She grabbed her robe and pulled it on over her shorty pj's before opening the door. "What's wrong?"

"I wanted to talk and I heard you on the phone. Who was calling so late?"

She stiffened until she realized that of course he had the right to ask that kind of question. What could she say? She looked into his warm brown eyes, alight with love and concern for her. How could she put him through what that evil man demanded? Couldn't they work through this together? Wasn't that what married couples did?

He took a step closer, and his warm palm enveloped her cheek. She closed her eyes and relished the heat that spread down her neck to her belly. She loved him so much. How could she go on with this lie? Because that's what it was. Withholding the full truth was just as much a lie.

He rubbed his thumb over her skin. "I know you love me, Leia. Even now I can feel it. I have your ring in my pocket. Let's put it back on your finger."

She opened her eyes and studied him. Everything in her warred over what to do. "I can't do that, Bane. I wish I could. Th-There's . . ."

He dropped his hand and turned away before she could get out the words she needed to say. He moved toward the door, but she grabbed his arm and spun him around. When he turned to face her, she threw her arms around his neck and pressed her lips against his. She needed to feel his passion, needed his strength and wisdom.

He stood still for a moment, then his arms went around her waist, and he pulled her close. The stubble on his face rasped against the tender skin of her face, but she didn't care.

Heat flared over her skin, and he wrapped his hand through the loose hair trailing down to her waist. Her hands clutched his shirt and she closed her eyes and willed herself to forget the dire circumstances, just for a minute. All that mattered in the moment was his warm breath mingling with hers and the firm assurance of his embrace.

She made a small sound of protest when his lips left hers, then opened her eyes. His expression was hard to read in the dimly lit room.

He retreated a few feet. "What's going on, Leia? One minute you push me away and the next you're kissing me l-like that."

She inhaled, knowing in that moment she couldn't live without him. "Eva's been kidnapped."

~ɔℓℓₑ~

Bane shook his head to clear it. "What are you talking about?"

He couldn't take his eyes off her with her brown hair spilling over her shoulders. He'd loved her for so long, but since this afternoon, he wasn't sure he knew her as well as he thought he did. His lips still tingled from her kiss. He stared into her blue eyes, so filled with pain.

Kidnapped.

She wet her lips. "That was the kidnapper."

There was more she wasn't telling him. She should have run to his room the minute the guy called. Instead, he'd had to find her and she was still in her room. Almost like she'd hidden it from him.

She stepped toward him. "That's the real reason I broke our engagement. The kidnapper told me if I didn't, h-he'd kill Eva." She bit her trembling lip.

He put his hand on his head and took a step toward her. "Wait, let me get this straight. You took a call earlier today and instead of telling me about it, you broke our engagement?"

Her eyes on him, she nodded. "He threatened to kill Eva if I told you."

Raking a hand through his hair, he paced toward the window. "And you believed him? You didn't trust me enough to tell me the truth? Instead, you flippantly break my heart and push me away."

He'd been in the Coast Guard, for Pete's sake. Danger was nothing new to him. Who would be better equipped to find Eva than him? Leia must not trust him at all.

She held her hand out toward him. "It's not that at all! This is my sister's life we're talking about. He was very specific about what I had to do if I wanted to see her again."

She was so beautiful standing there in her white robe with her feet bare and her hair loose. Another week and she would be his bride. Naturally she'd been upset when this guy called.

She should have told me.

He took her hand. "Tell me exactly what he said."

She tucked a long lock behind her ear. "His voice was electronically garbled. He said I was not to call the police, and that if I told you, we'd find Eva's body in the sea." Her voice wobbled. "Then he said I had to break the engagement if I ever wanted to see Eva again."

"This guy has something personal against me. I bet it's Zimmer."

"Who's Zimmer?"

"A scumbag I sent to jail for robbery and manslaughter. He swore he'd get revenge." He watched her flinch. "My tires were slashed this afternoon. Two of them."

"You're sure it was him?"

"Who else?" He stared at her and wished all his doubts could be erased with a kiss. "Before today, I would have sworn you believed in me, trusted me with your life."

"I do!"

He made himself take her outstretched hand. She was dealing with enough upset today. "You should have come to me immediately. We looked for her all afternoon until dark. Yet you didn't say a word. It was all a lie. You knew she wasn't out there, yet you let me and the Coast Guard waste our time when we could have been looking for the kidnapper."

Her eyes welled and tears slipped down her face. "You're right. I was just so scared, Bane. I couldn't bear it if my actions hurt Eva. He sounded so—so deadly, and I was sure he would kill her on the spot if I didn't agree to his demands."

Her tears melted his anger, and he pulled her against his chest. "I wouldn't have shut you out like this."

"You don't understand! This is Eva. She's like a child. You know she's scared. I just want her back." She began to sob. "I know I should have told you, but I panicked. And I'm telling you now. I could have still kept it from you, but I didn't."

He smoothed her hair, fragrant with the scent of ginger, and pressed his lips against her temple. "I'm worried about Eva too. What did he say just now when he called?"

"He said he knew we didn't cancel the food order. If it's not canceled by noon, he'll kill her."

Bane stilled as he thought through what that meant. "So he's checking up on you."

She nodded. "I told him I'd cancel it at nine when they opened."

"So why tell me now?"

"I realized I was wrong," she whispered. "I can't handle this by myself. We have to find her. I can't trust that he'll keep his word."

He nodded. "We can't trust anything Zimmer says. We have to find her." Bane wheeled toward the door. "We'd better call the police."

"But what if he finds out? He'll kill her!"

He turned slowly back to face her as he thought about it. The guy did seem to be anticipating their every move, and he knew they hadn't canceled the food order. "Let me talk to Mano and Kaia about it."

He walked out the door and into the hallway. He'd have to wake up Kaia and Jesse.

FOUR

EVA SAT WITH HER FEET DANGLING INTO THE WATER. The tile decking was warm under her, and she felt a little sleepy. "Leia would like this pool." She smiled up at her new friend Chris.

Chris smiled back. "I'll invite her over."

Eva straightened and smiled. "When? I want to see her. I'm not used to her being gone. When did she say she'd be back?"

"In a few days."

Eva pooched out her lip. "She usually takes me with her."

Chris sat beside her. "I know, but you can't expect to go with her on her honeymoon. That wouldn't be fair."

Fair. Eva hadn't considered fair. "I was supposed to be in the wedding. It wasn't fair they did it without me."

"Bane was going to have to go to a new job."

Eva had heard all of that already, and it didn't make it any better that she'd been excluded. She swished her feet in the warm water and watched the swirling eddies around her toes. "There's no Christmas tree here. There should be a tree and decorations. It's the holiest holiday of all."

"I don't like Christmas." His voice was gruff.

"You have to like Christmas. Jesus was born. I love Jesus."

"Quit talking about it! There's no Christmas here."

"I don't want to talk to you anymore. You're being mean to me when I just want to see my sister." She folded her arms across her chest. Just because Chris had bought her a new bathing suit and some shorts didn't mean anything when her heart ached to see Leia.

Chris stood. "Suit yourself."

Eva didn't look up when the door to the house banged. There was a fence all the way 'round the yard, but maybe she could still get out. If she couldn't see Leia, she could stay with Kaia. She liked Kaia and Nani, the coolest dolphin ever. She was almost human and liked swimming with her. Eva pulled her legs out of the water and stood. Glancing toward the door, she saw Chris wasn't around. She picked up her towel and wrapped it around her waist.

She trailed her fingers along the fence, hoping to find a gate. Didn't all fences have a gate somewhere? But the solid fence was six feet high and without an opening. To get out, she'd have to go through the house. Maybe Chris would be in the bathroom or bedroom. Eva went to the back door and opened it as noiselessly as she could.

Chris's voice echoed over the tiled floors. "I think we should kill her. She's driving me crazy."

Terror gripped Eva's throat. She tiptoed over the marble floors toward the front door. Ice clinked in a glass in the kitchen on the other side of the fireplace wall. Hopefully, Chris thought she was still outside. She unlocked the door and opened it, freezing when it made a squeak. The sound of soda pouring into a glass reassured her, and she eased open the door, then stepped out onto the wide plantation-style porch.

"Eva?" Chris's voice was still distant.

Not bothering to shut the door behind her, Eva bolted for the walk that went to the front gate. She wrestled with the lock, then realized she had to have a key to get out.

"Eva?" Chris was right behind her.

She whirled with her back to the gate. "I-I heard you! You said you wanted to kill me. I don't want to be dead. I don't like you anymore. You need to let me go before Bane comes. He'll be mad at you."

She lashed out a hand as Chris reached for her.

Leia, surrounded by Bane's family, sat at a secluded table on the patio at Joe's on the Green. Christmas music on steel guitars played over the loudspeakers. "My Hawaiian Christmas" was just ending. She picked listlessly at her eggs and Spam.

Bane's shoulder brushed hers as he reached for his coffee. "I canceled the food."

"I called the florist," Kaia said. "What else?"

"The tents?" her husband, Jesse, suggested. He was a navy officer and spoke in a clipped, no-nonsense voice. His blond hair gleamed in the sunshine.

"I took care of that," Annie said. Her quiet competence, inherited from her Japanese mother, usually calmed those around her.

It did Leia's heart good to see the way they all rallied around her. Kaia hadn't scolded her for keeping the phone call from her, though Leia had glimpsed hurt in her eyes when she heard the news. Didn't they understand this was her sister's life at risk? Surely they would have done the same thing.

She realized they were all staring at her. "Sorry, did I miss something?"

Bane slipped his arm around her. "I know it's rough on you, honey. Kaia just mentioned the guy called you shortly after he and Eva had evidently jumped off the cliff. That seems to indicate more than one person is involved."

She nodded, relaxing into his embrace. At least he wasn't acting as upset with her. "I wondered about that too."

Mano shook his head. "Not necessarily. I've jumped that cliff plenty of times, and I'm back to shore in five minutes. If he left his cell phone on the beach and called as soon as he got back, the timing would work."

"But why did Eva go with him? No one heard her scream," Annie said.

Bane's fingers tightened around Leia's arm. "You haven't been around Eva much. She trusts everyone. If he gave her a present, even a candy bar, and was nice to her, she'd think they were best buddies."

Annie winced and stared at Leia with sympathy in her eyes. "I bet it's hard to watch out for her in today's world."

"It wasn't quite so hard on Moloka'i. We know everyone, and there aren't many visitors to our area. It's very different here with so many tourists."

"We'll find her," Jesse said, his blue eyes intense. "I've informed the navy base to be on the lookout for her, and I've instructed our patrols to keep an eye out when on the water."

"D-Did you call the police? The kidnapper specifically said no police."

She glanced around the full patio. Could he be here even now watching her? She edged away from Bane. When he lifted a brow, she shrugged. "He might be watching. We're not supposed to be engaged any longer."

His lips flattened, but he pulled his arm back and moved away a few inches. "I didn't call them yet. We have resources to tap ourselves first, just in case he has a mole in the police department."

Mano leaned forward on his muscular forearms. "I'm going to go to the local hotels and ask around."

"And I know some real-estate people who rent to tourists. I'm going to get a list of single male renters and scope out the units."

Leia frowned. "What if there's more than one person involved?"

"You mean like a couple?" Kaia's eyes widened. "You're right. I should probably stake out every condo complex and ask for a list of rental houses."

"It's like looking for a mongoose in the weeds," Annie put in. "There are so many rental units on the island."

"I bet he's close by, though," Bane said. "He's keeping an eye on Leia. So we should only have to check out the South Shore rentals."

"I'll start with the ones on Hoona and Lawai Roads. Lots of tourists out that way, and it's quiet. A perfect place for someone to hide out," Mano said. "Some of the big homes out by Kukui'ula Harbor are rentals, and they are very private."

"And expensive," Kaia added.

Her brother shrugged. "Whoever put this plan together has some money. It wasn't cheap to pull this off. The ticket alone would have been a thousand dollars. Add lodging, food, and rental car, and you're up to a good three grand or more."

"What about up along Omao Road? Some of those places are very private with long lanes back into the trees," Bane said.

"I'll add that to the list." Mano rose. "Annie, you come with me. We'll get a list and see what we can find out."

Annie stood but paused long enough to touch Leia's shoulder. "Try not to worry, honey. We'll get to the bottom of this."

Leia nodded. "*Mahalo* for giving me hope."

"You're one of us." Kaia rose as well. "We Oanas stick together."

The rest of the family murmured agreement as they headed out to scour the island. Leia took the last sip of her coffee. "What are we going to do?"

Bane shrugged. "It will have to be separate, though I don't like it. I don't trust this guy. He seems to be watching, though, and if we go anywhere together, he's bound to think you aren't following the rules. I'm going to follow my hunch and have the police try to find Zimmer."

He held up his hand when she opened her mouth to object. "This will not appear to have anything to do with Eva. The guy slashed my tires. When someone flies in from the mainland, they have to put on their agricultural form where they're staying and for how long. I'm hoping to track that down. It will give us some place to start."

"I didn't realize there was a form like that, but then I've never been to the mainland." She allowed a tiny spark of hope to hover in her chest. "That would be wonderful if the form said where he was staying and we had Eva back by evening!"

"I'll do all I can." Bane started to lean forward to kiss her, then checked himself. "You could walk through the area around Shipwreck in case he has her in one of the condos or rentals around Poipu Kai. She might call out to you."

"Even though she's willing to be friends with anyone, she'll be asking for me." Her eyes filled with tears. "We have to find her before another night goes by."

Five

Eva rubbed her arm where Chris had grabbed her. Though she kicked and screamed, he dragged her back into the house, then locked her in her room. The window was nailed shut from the outside. The bedroom wasn't for a kid like her. It was dark and dingy with a faded flowered spread. The floor was tile but it didn't look like it had been washed in a while. Leia would have gotten her mop out the minute she saw it.

Eva rubbed her wet eyes and rocked back and forth with her arms clasped around herself. She wanted her sister.

The door opened and Chris poked his head inside. She tensed before she realized he was smiling. She returned his smile tentatively. At least if he was smiling, he wasn't going to hurt her again.

"Hungry?"

Her stomach growled at the word, and she nodded. "Can I come out?"

"You promise not to try to run away again?"

She rubbed her arm. "You hurt me." She didn't like him anymore. Not even when he smiled.

His smile faded. "It was your own fault, Eva. I told you the rules. You didn't obey them, now did you?"

She hung her head. "No." Rules were important. But what if the rules were mean like his? What would Leia tell her to do?

"If you're going to be good, you can come out and eat now. I bought you some cereal."

She rose from the bed and went toward the door. "Leia fixes me eggs with runny yolks. I don't like cereal."

"Well, that's all we've got. Don't be so demanding." He gave her a shove out the door.

She scurried ahead of him to the small kitchen. At least the cereal had chocolate in it. Maybe it wouldn't be too bad. While she got down a bowl from the cabinet and pulled the milk from the fridge, he walked over and looked out the window. There weren't any other houses around. She didn't know Kaua'i very well, so she didn't know where they were. Bane had said the west side was warmer and had fewer people. Maybe that's where they were. But no, the flowers and plants in the yard were nice and green, and she hadn't seen any cactus.

Even if she'd gotten away, she wouldn't have known where to run. She forced herself to take a spoonful of cereal, but it sat like sand in her mouth. He'd be mad if she spit it out, so she managed to chew and swallow while she watched him. What if he hurt her again? She didn't like him anymore.

He saw her staring. "What? You look like you'd like to stick me with that spoon."

She folded her arms over her chest. "You're not my friend anymore."

He grinned. "Honey, I was never your friend. You're the means to an end."

She didn't know what that meant, but she didn't like his sneer. "I used to like you."

"Yeah, well, I never liked you. I'm going to make your sister and her boyfriend pay for what they did to me." He went past her to the living room.

The sunlight reflected off something metallic on the counter. His cell phone! She glanced into the living room. His back was to the doorway as he aimed the remote at the TV. She slipped from her chair and grabbed the phone, then stuck it in her bra. Returning to the table, she gulped down the rest of the tasteless cereal, then went to the doorway.

"I'm done eating now. I'm going to go to my room."

"Fine." He didn't turn around as he changed channels.

Her bare feet fairly flew down the hall, and she shut the door behind her. She tried to lock it, but he'd broken the lock on the inside. She went to the far corner and punched in her sister's number. Her pulse throbbed in her neck as it rang.

"Hello?"

The sound of Leia's voice brought tears surging to Eva's eyes. "Leia? It's me. You have to come get me. He's being mean now. I'm sorry I went with him." Her voice broke. "You told me to be careful, but he seemed so nice at first."

"Eva! Where are you, honey? I'll come get you."

"I don't know. In a house. There aren't other houses around. You have to come get me. I want to go home." She started to cry, hiccuping sounds that would bring him in to yell at her. Swallowing back the sobs, she peered out the window. He'd be so mad if he knew she'd called her sister.

"Whose phone is this?" Leia sounded in charge and confident.

"It's his. I found it on the counter. He'll be missing it soon so I have to take it back. He'll hurt me again if he sees me with it. Come get me, Leia."

"I will, honey. We're looking for you. Don't go. What do you see out the window?"

Eva heard a noise in the hall. The doorknob began to turn. "He's coming!" She clicked off the phone and turned to face him.

ꕯꕯꕯ

The Java Kai coffee shop in Kapaa was hopping as usual, and the streets were filled with Christmas shoppers. Bane ordered a large black coffee and a Maui Mocha, then grabbed a newly vacated table outside. He'd just sat down when he spied his friend heading up the walk. "Ron, over here. I've got your mocha already."

Ron Parker was a tall whip of a man with a shock of amazingly red hair and strong features. He was out of uniform today in jeans and a black T-shirt with a Dodgers baseball cap on backward. His smile was genuine when he spotted Bane.

Bane slid the coffee drink across the table to where Ron was seated. "You remembered, brah."

"Hard to forget a coffee drink that has coconut in it."

Ron's grin faded. "I heard about your soon-to-be sister-in-law's drowning. I'm sorry."

Bane badly wanted to tell his friend the truth, but he bit back the confession. "*Mahalo*. We're still holding out hope she turns up. She's a really good swimmer."

"That's encouraging." Ron took a cautious sip of the hot mocha. "You said you needed my help?"

Bane nodded and leaned forward in his chair. "Did you see the report about my tires getting slashed yesterday?"

Ron shook his head. "I've been off the last couple of days. We don't see much vandalism on the island. Where did it happen?"

"In front of Tomkats."

"Wow, that's bold. Broad daylight?"

Bane nodded. "Town was a little deserted, though."

"Sundays can be that way this time of year. The biggest influx of tourists will start in another day or two." He took another sip of his mocha. "You ask around to see if anyone saw the perp?"

Bane nodded. "Called police headquarters too, and an officer came out. No one seemed to see anything."

Ron eyed Bane. "Sounds like you have a suspect in mind. How can I help?"

"A man I helped convict for robbery and manslaughter got out of prison last week. He has carried a grudge against me a long time. I believe he's on the island. I'd like you to see if you can get hold of his agriculture form to see where he's staying." Bane told him about Zimmer.

"Whoa, buddy, you don't need to confront an excon. That is a job for me and mine."

He would have to confide in Ron. They had gone to

school together and had been friends since first grade. Bane could only pray Ron kept it to himself. "There's more, but you can't tell headquarters."

Ron put his cup down. "I don't think I can promise that. Do you know about another crime?"

Bane exhaled and sat back in his chair. "If you tell anyone, someone I love could lose her life. I need you to promise me, brah."

Ron's green eyes widened. "Is this about Eva?"

He should have known Ron would guess. The man was no slouch when it came to investigations. "Yeah. She's been kidnapped. Leia has received a total of two calls from the kidnapper. He told her she had to break our engagement or he'd kill Eva."

"I see why you think it's Zimmer then. This is someone with a personal vendetta." Ron's expression hardened. "I bet Eva's terrified."

"I don't know. She's very trusting, and if the guy is nice to her, she'll take it with a smile. Leia's a mess, though. And Eva will start missing her family very soon. I have to find her."

Ron tapped his fingers on the table. "And if he listed his address on the form . . ."

"Exactly. We can find him and rescue Eva."

"I'll get a warrant for that form. Buddy, you really should have reported this. The entire force was out last night looking for her. The officers won't be happy they were misled."

"They weren't! I didn't know myself until early this morning."

"Leia didn't even tell you? Whoa."

Bane picked up his cup. "Yeah, can't say I was happy about it. Kind of a slap in the face." He hadn't wanted to admit his feelings to his siblings because he wanted them to love Leia. It felt safer somehow to talk to his longtime friend. "I gotta be honest—it's starting to make me wonder how much she really loves and trusts me."

Ron's gaze was sober when he nodded. "I can understand that. You talk to her about this?"

"Not much. She was already upset about Eva, and I didn't want to add to it."

"Brah, it'll have to get out in the open. The last thing you want is to go into a marriage that isn't right."

"I know. Once we find Eva, we'll talk it out and I'll decide what to do."

"So the wedding is off for now?"

Bane nodded. "That was the kidnapper's main demand, and he is checking up on her. He called her at midnight and told her he knew we hadn't canceled the food order."

"How'd he know where you'd ordered the catering?"

Bane shrugged. "No idea. Maybe he called around. There aren't that many catering places on the island."

"Or maybe it's not Zimmer at all. It could be someone local."

Bane hadn't even considered it could be someone else. "Like who?"

"Hard to say." Ron swallowed the last of his coffee. "I'll do some digging."

"And keep it to yourself?"

He stood and turned his cap around the right way. "For now. But if we haven't found her in the next few hours, I'll have to ask for help. You know the first few hours of a kidnapping are critical. I don't feel good about not reporting it even now."

"I know." Bane rose and tossed his cup into the trash. "Give me until morning."

SIX

THE BACK OF LEIA'S NECK PRICKLED, AND SHE WHIRLED on the sidewalk along the back side of the Grand Hyatt by the ocean. The hotel had brought out all kinds of Christmas decorations, from giant wreaths to towering snowmen. A few tourists looked at her from their lounges around the saltwater lagoon, then went back to their books. She examined each one with care, but no one looked suspicious. She could have sworn someone was staring at her.

Where was her sister? She was frantic to find Eva after that phone call. Eva was so scared, and Leia felt helpless to rescue her. Maybe she should call the police. Even though the call had come up Unknown, the police might be able to trace it. But the man's threats left her frightened at the possible consequences.

She was hot and itchy from the sun, and the lagoon water looked refreshing. Averting her gaze, she resumed her stride toward Poipu Sands. The popular condos would be filled with tourists. She turned to walk to the lobby and heard her name. Turning, she saw Bane running toward her.

Her pulse leaped and she rushed to meet him. "You found her?"

He shook his head. "Sorry, honey. But I just got a call from Ron. He's got an address."

"Already?" She grabbed his hand, then realized they might be seen and quickly dropped it and stepped back. "Where?"

"A house in Poipu Kai, back along the green belt. Let's go."

It warmed her that he'd come to find her first without going straight there. Eva would need her if she became frightened. She hurried with him along the path to the houses fronting the green belt. Maybe Eva would be in her arms in just a few minutes.

They paused when they reached where the sidewalk split. "Do we have backup? What if he has a gun?"

Bane patted his pocket. "I'm prepared."

She looked around the green belt. Some people jogged along the walk, others strolled with their dogs on leashes. The lush vegetation shimmered with color

and fragrance, and Christmas lights adorned the shrub-
bery. The feeling of being watched persisted, but she
saw no one staring in their direction. The sea breeze
blew her hair into her face, and she plaited it while she
waited for Bane.

She followed him when he set off on the right fork
of the walk, toward Keleka Road where beautiful homes
lined the shaded streets. "He paid some bucks to rent
back in here."

"Yeah. Wonder where he got the money after being
in prison." Bane paused and surveyed the house, a single-story plantation style with a wide front porch and
beautiful vegetation in the yard. "There's a car in the
drive."

"I noticed." She wanted to march to the door and
demand her sister, but the wide windows would reveal
who stood on the porch. The guy was liable to appear
with a gun. She tugged on Bane's hand and pulled him
behind a large palm tree. "I don't want him to see us. I
think you should call Mano so you have backup."

Bane glanced at his cell when the text alert dinged.
"Ron just drove through Koloa so he'll be here in ten
minutes. He's going to meet us here. We can stake it out
while we wait."

Pacing seemed like a bad idea in case they were seen,
so to corral herself, she settled on the stiff, springy turf

and clasped her knees to her chest. "What did you tell Ron? He just thinks it's about vandalism, right?"

He shook his head. "I told him the truth. All of it."

Her stomach plunged. "I assumed you told him about the tire slashing. The kidnapper said no police."

His dark eyes were expressionless. "I had to tell Ron. He knew there was more going on than what I was revealing. I needed his help tracking down Zimmer. He wouldn't give me the address otherwise."

She got to her feet and brushed flecks of grass from her hands. "I trusted you not to tell them. See, this is why I kept it from you in the first place. You law enforcement types stick together. If Eva dies, it's your fault!"

Shaking, she started to walk away, but he grabbed her forearm. "That's a lousy thing to say, Leia. I'm trying to save your sister. I love her too, you know. Statistics show bringing in the police is the best way to retrieve a kidnapped victim. You think you're capable of getting her back by yourself? I thought that's why you finally told me. You knew you couldn't do it alone. Well, I can't do it alone either."

He was right. His touch on her arm made her skin tingle. She pressed herself against him and buried her face in his shirt. His heart pounded hard under her ear. She tipped her face up to his. "I'm sorry, but I'm so scared."

His hand smoothed her hair. "Shh, shh. It's going to be all right, Leia." His lips brushed hers.

Her hands bunched into his shirt, and she kissed him back, drawing in the strength she needed. Bane was here. His sheer force of will would make sure Eva survived this.

He lifted his head and cupped her face in his hands. "As soon as Ron gets here, we'll go in. She'll be back with us very soon."

She nodded. "We have to move fast. She called me just before you came to get me and said he'd hurt her."

His hand fell away. "Wait a minute. Eva called you? Why didn't you tell me? How badly is she hurt?"

"We had a lead, so that was more important." She bit her lip. "I think he just squeezed her arm. She sounded panicked but okay."

"What'd she say? Did she give you any clues on her whereabouts?"

She shook her head. "She said there were no other houses around, so it was somewhere out of town. There are close neighbors here. She sounded so scared and kept begging me to come get her." Her voice broke. "She's depending on me to save her, and I'm so afraid he'll kill her if we don't do what he says."

Her cell phone rang, and her heart plunged when she pulled it out and looked at the screen. *Unknown.*

"It's him." She swallowed hard, then answered the call. "Hello."

A scream reverberated through the phone, then her sister cried out, "Leia, help me!"

"Eva!" Her sister's voice was loud enough for Bane to hear too. "Let her go!"

He winced and looked toward the house. *I'm going in*, he mouthed.

She shook her head and held up one finger. He'd need backup. "Are you there?"

"Just remember, everything that happens from here on out is your fault," the electronic voice said. "You're with Bane now, aren't you? You told him, didn't you? All the wedding cancellations were just a trick to throw me off, but I'm too smart for you."

The phone went dead. Leia stared up at Bane. "He's hurting her! I bet he caught her with his cell phone."

Bane looked over her shoulder. "There's Ron. We're going in. Stay here."

"I'm coming with you!"

Ron's car door opened and he got out. "This the house?" His gaze flicked to Leia, then back to Bane.

Bane nodded. "And Leia just got a call from Eva. She was screaming." His jaw flexed and his eyes narrowed. "He'll pay for that."

Leia could still hear her sister's screams. "Let me go to the door first. You two can circle around the back. I don't think he'll feel threatened if I go up alone."

Bane began to shake his head but Ron nodded. "Makes sense. We'll wait until you're inside. Keep him away from the back of the house if you can."

"I don't want her hurt," Bane said.

"I'm not going to stand here and argue. I want my sister back." *Please, God, let her be okay.*

Leia headed up the driveway with more confidence than she felt. Keeping her gaze fastened on the door, she marched up the steps and rang the bell.

At first there was no answer. She rang again, then rapped hard on the door.

"Coming," a gruff voice called out.

The door swung open, and she saw a burly man about six feet tall. He had thick black hair that was unruly as though he'd just gotten out of bed, though it was afternoon. He wore a T-shirt and loose-fitting denim shorts. His feet were bare. She thought he was probably in his early forties.

"I've come for my sister."

His hazel eyes clouded. "Your sister? Who the heck are you? There's no woman here."

"You're Dennis Zimmer, right?"

He nodded. "So what?"

"You kidnapped my sister. I know she's in there, and I want her back right now."

He held up his hands. "Kidnapping? Whoa, listen, I've turned over a new leaf. In fact, I'm only here to apologize to a guy. I don't know anything about a kidnapping."

She believed him. Her heart sank. "Then you won't mind if I look around the house and make sure?"

He stepped out of the way. "Suit yourself. You won't find anyone here but me."

~∂℃~

Bees buzzed around the pikake and gardenias lining the wide plantation porch, and the scent of flowers filled the air. Bane stood on the wide porch with his hands in the pockets of his shorts. He couldn't deny he was tense just being in Zimmer's presence, even though Leia assured him he didn't have anything to do with Eva's disappearance.

Zimmer stood by the door, next to the Aloha sign hanging on the siding. He looked older and more sober than the last time. Prison had changed him. Gone was the devil-may-care light in his eyes and the contemptuous sneer he usually wore.

Leia touched Bane's arm. "He has something to say to you."

Zimmer took a deep breath. "Yeah, I just want to tell you I'm glad I went to prison. So I came here to thank you for making sure I paid for my crimes."

Bane blinked. "I don't get it. You swore to get even with me for sending you there."

Zimmer shuffled a little in his bare feet. "I know, and I'm sorry. I was a different man then. I've changed. Started going to a Bible study at the prison and, well, I see things differently now. I caused harm to a lot of people, and I can't make amends for most of what I did, especially for Dalton's death."

Ron was beside Bane, and he glanced at his friend but said nothing.

Bane nodded. "Have you seen his family?"

Zimmer winced, his hazel eyes filling with pain. "Yeah, his wife didn't want to hear anything I had to say. I don't blame her. Not much I can do to bring her husband back."

The guy seemed genuine. "I'm glad to hear you've changed. How long are you here for?"

"A week. Figured if I was going to spend the money to come, I'd see the island."

Where had he gotten that kind of money? "You here alone?"

"Yeah, though I'm seeing someone. She's coming tomorrow and staying in a condo on Shipwreck Beach. She paid for my trip." He looked down at the floor. "She, uh, she's my lawyer, and she had a lot to do with turning my life around."

The last of Bane's suspicions melted away. "I hope you have a great trip. We'd better be going, though. We still need to find Eva." He took Leia's hand, and they started down the steps with Ron on their heels.

They reached Ron's car. "I was sure he'd slashed my tires. You think it was a random act, Ron?"

Ron shook his head. "Anything's on the table now."

"It happened the afternoon Eva was kidnapped, so it seemed likely they might be related."

"And it's the reason you assumed whoever has done this is after you, right?"

Bane nodded. "So it's possible I was on the wrong trail all along. Actually, I was since I thought it was Zimmer who slashed my tires."

Ron glanced at Leia, who'd been unnaturally quiet. "You have any enemies, Leia? Where are you from?"

Leia's fingers curled more tightly around Bane's. "I live on Moloka'i. I don't have any enemies I know of."

Ron shrugged. "Okay, it was just a thought. I'll poke around and see if I can find out anything."

Bane looked back at the house. "You know it's not

entirely true you have no enemies, Leia. We share a couple of common enemies from that fiasco about the artifacts. The henchmen might be out of jail now. Their sentences were lighter."

She went white, then nodded. "Moe Fletcher and Gene Chambers. Can we find out if they're out of jail?"

Ron nodded. "Let me make a call."

Bane glanced back toward the house. "They were in the same prison as Zimmer. Let's see if he met either of them. Wait here. He might know something about them."

Birds chirped from the avocado trees as he hurried back to the house. Zimmer was sitting at the lanai table and rose when he saw him.

Bane stopped on the bottom step. "I had one more question. I thought of someone who hates both of us, and I wouldn't be surprised if they were already out of prison. Did you meet Moe Fletcher or Gene Chambers?"

Zimmer's eyes widened. "Fletcher was my cell mate. Bad character, very bad. We got into a few scuffles, and I thought he'd kill me in my sleep some night."

"Is he still there?"

Zimmer shook his head. "He was released the month before me." His mouth hardened. "He talked about making a couple pay for putting him behind bars. That wouldn't be the two of you, would it?"

"Probably. I'll see if I can find out if he's on the

island. *Mahalo* for your help." Bane bounded down the steps to the walk.

"I'll call if I hear anything. I know the kinds of places he's apt to hang out," Zimmer called after him.

Fletcher would pay for hurting Eva.

SEVEN

BANE WAS QUIET AS THEY DROVE TOWARD LIHUE TO meet with Ron. Leia gazed out the window at the mountains rising on either side of the road as they left the tree tunnel. A light rain splattered the windshield, and she pressed her forehead against the glass. Dark clouds rolled in atop the mountaintops, and the wind picked up, stirring the palm fronds and the monkey-pod tree leaves. The weathermen had predicted a cold front with accompanying rain. She could only pray Eva was safely inside somewhere. Her sister's screams reverberated in her head. Was she being tortured? Was she dead?

Leia couldn't tell what Bane was thinking. He'd been different since he found out she'd kept the kidnapper's call from him. Still concerned and solicitous but in a remote way, as if she was just another woman he was trying to help.

She turned back around to look at him. He stared straight ahead at the road. "Talk to me, Bane."

He glanced from the road, then back. "What do you want to talk about?"

The lump in her throat felt like a conch shell. "Us. There is still an us, isn't there?"

He drummed his fingers on the steering wheel, then shrugged. "You sure you want to get into this now, Leia?" His voice was tight as though he had hold of his emotions in a death grip.

"We have a twenty-minute drive before we get to the police station, so yes. We have time to discuss the way you've hardly looked at me or touched me, let alone kissed me. If I touch you, you kiss me back, but you haven't initiated anything." She laid her hand on his arm and could feel the response through his skin. He might not want her touch to mean anything, but it still did.

She wished the car were stopped so she could grab him by the shoulders and *make* him look her in the eye. She wanted to see into his heart, into the depths of his soul the way she used to.

He pressed his lips together, then exhaled. "It's been hard getting past being abandoned again."

Her cheeks burned as if he'd slapped her. "I never abandoned you."

"It felt like it. It was my mother all over again. One minute she was there and the next she'd run off with some guy. The way I saw things changed. I thought she loved me, then she walked away."

She removed her hand from his arm and clasped her hands together in her lap to keep them from trembling. "What does that have to do with Eva's kidnapping?"

They passed several houses decorated for Christmas, the lights shining out in the storm. Christmas. This felt like anything but Christmas. He still hadn't answered her. "Bane?"

His jaw clenched. "You shut me out the same way. I realized I didn't know you as well as I thought I did. Just like my mother, you were hiding things from me. If you want the truth of it, I'm hurt, Leia. Hurt you wouldn't tell me your deepest fears and feelings, and I'm afraid of what that means. I thought we had a bond that was special. Now I find it wasn't anything nearly as unique as I thought. We have passion, not denying that. Anytime you touch me, I want you close. But passion is nothing without trust."

Her eyes burned, and the boulder in her throat grew. She'd never thought how this might hurt him. "I'm sorry, Bane. I panicked. Can't you understand how that could happen?"

"Your first inclination should have been to turn to me, but it wasn't. And that kills me inside, just kills me." His voice was low and hoarse.

He shot a glance her way, and she nearly groaned from the pain in his eyes. What had she done? "I love you, Bane. You know I do. I'm only whole when we're together. It was my first inclination to talk to you, but I was so scared of what he might do. I wanted to tell you."

He grimaced. "It doesn't look that way, babe."

At least he was still calling her babe. "Do you love me?"

He gripped the wheel so tightly his knuckles went white. "You know I do. But what kind of marriage will we have if I'm always worried you're going to run out on me like my mom?"

She reached over and touched his forearm. It was rock hard from his grip on the steering wheel. "I would never leave you! You have to know that."

He shot her another look. "Do I? You sent me away once before. And you haven't exactly been pushing to get to the 'I dos.' This has been the longest engagement on record."

"It's only been a year." When she moved her hand to his face, he flinched a little. She brushed his thick black hair out of his eyes. "You're my world, Bane. I can't lose you. Please, you have to understand. I panicked, pure and simple. It made sense to follow what he said to get Eva back."

"Did it?" At least he didn't move his head away. "I'll have to take some time and think about this. There hasn't been an opportunity with our search for Eva. Right now, I guess you could say the wedding is truly off unless I can wrap my head around all of this."

She let her hand fall away as she absorbed the shock. On one level she understood his hurt, but why couldn't he see this was her *sister*, a sister who was really a child in spite of her actual age? "You don't think my first responsibility should have been to Eva?"

He skewered her with a glance. "We are supposed to be one. You split us into two when you shut me out. That's rejection, Leia. I'm trying to assimilate it, but it's hard to swallow."

An unspoken *if ever* hovered between them. The hurt went deep in him, deeper than she'd realized. All his childhood abandonment pain had resurged, and it was her fault.

～ﾟﾟ～

Christmas revelers lined Rice Street waiting for the parade and the kickoff of the annual Festival of Lights.

The sun hung low in the sky, and Bane drove on through town out to Kalapaki Bay where they were to meet with Ron. He parked down the street.

Leia hadn't said much after they'd talked. He still felt raw and unsettled. There had been tears in her eyes, and he had to admit his heart had leaped when she said she loved him. And he knew she did, in her own way maybe. But he no longer was sure her kind of love was the lasting kind that would see them through ups and downs. At least it didn't appear to be.

He pulled the key from the ignition and glanced at her from the corner of his eye. Her long brown hair was in a braid that hung over one shoulder. He'd hoped to see it spill over a white nightgown on their wedding night. That might not happen now.

He opened his door. "Ron said he'd meet us at his house just down the street. We'll walk instead of park in his drive, just in case it tips off the kidnapper."

"There he is." Leia pointed out Ron standing along the side of the road.

When Ron saw he had their attention, he started off at a brisk pace down the street. They waited a couple of minutes, then followed. When he entered a small single-story house, they went up the walk and rang the bell.

He opened it immediately and ushered them into a small living room. The sofa and chairs were leather, and seashells and other beach decor lightened the dark furniture. A small Christmas tree was on a table by the window. The seashell decorations were all white.

"Have a seat." He motioned to the sofa. "I have a lead on your guys. They both arrived here last week from Honolulu. They did not fill out the line of the form with their location here, but Fletcher has a cousin who lives here." Ron held up his hand when Bane started to speak. "The cousin lives in Waimea. Even if Fletcher's not there, we might get a lead on his whereabouts."

Bane frowned. "But wouldn't his probation officer have to know where he is?"

"You'd think so, but I called his probation officer. He had no idea Fletcher or Chambers left O'ahu."

"So they're both in violation of probation," Leia said.

"Yep. Which is good for us. I ordered a warrant for their arrest for violation of parole." Ron's voice was grim. "I've got an officer on his way to the house now."

Leia leaped to her feet. "What? I want to be there to protect Eva. You should have called us and told us to head that way instead of here."

"Calm down," Ron said. "All the guy is going to do is ask if the cousin's heard from Fletcher. It will be all about probation. The other reason I didn't send you that way is I read the report of a brawl in a bar here in town last night. The perp who started the fight escaped, but his description sounds a lot like Fletcher. And I have a picture from the surveillance footage at the bar." He pulled out his iPhone and showed a photo to them.

Bane took one look and nodded. "That's Fletcher all right. So he's here in Lihue?"

"Maybe. But I don't think he's in Waimea. Could be in Kapaa." Ron's cell phone rang, and he answered. "Parker." He listened, drumming his fingers on his knee, then he pulled a pen and pad from his pocket and jotted down something. "Got it, *mahalo.*" He grinned and punched his phone. "We got him. The cousin said Fletcher was staying with a friend here in Lihue. A condo complex about ten minutes away."

Leia looked toward the door. "Let's go!"

Ron nodded. "We'd better hurry. My boss thinks Fletcher knows he's been spotted. He might take her and run."

She grabbed Bane's hand and tugged him up, and he couldn't stop the surge of emotion filling his chest at her touch. If he could, he would rip these feelings out, but it would be harder than he imagined to root out the love. Maybe he never would.

He pulled his hand away and followed her out the door.

The sun was setting over the water when they exited the house. A car turned the corner and drove toward them. The blue Chrysler's headlamps came on, then the tires squealed as the driver tromped on the accelerator. The car sped toward them. At first Bane wasn't concerned, then the vehicle veered as though it was going to jump the curb and careen down the sidewalk.

He grabbed Leia's hand and shoved her toward the trees. "Run!"

He raced after her toward a large monkeypod tree festooned with lights. The engine whined behind him, and he heard a thump. Glancing behind, he saw the car leap the curb and head toward the field where they were. "He's trying to run us down!"

He grabbed Leia and propelled her faster to the huge tree trunk. They both clung to the backside of the tree. When he peered around the tree, he stared straight into the face of the man they sought—Moe Fletcher. A maniacal grin stretched across his face.

The car barely missed the tree, then zoomed away. But not before Bane caught a glimpse of white-blond hair and Eva's terrified eyes.

EIGHT

LEIA WAS SHAKING AS BANE HELPED HER UP. "I THINK I saw Eva! Is that possible?"

Bane nodded, his mouth a grim line. "I saw her clearly." His gun out, Ron ran toward them as the car careened around the corner. "Are you all right? Did you see the driver?"

Leia nodded, still shuddering at the look on his face. "It was Fletcher." She clasped her arms around herself.

"Let's go! We might be able to catch him." Ron motioned for them to jump in his car with him.

Bane got into the backseat with her. "You're trembling." He put his arm around her. But there was no real warmth in the embrace, at least none Leia could detect. It was like being hugged by a brother or a friend. He'd pulled out all the stops to put up a barrier between them, but she *knew* he still loved her. Even though they were close to getting Eva back, Leia wanted to bury her face in her hands and cry. What would her life be like without Bane in it? It would be like never being able to sit on the sand with the sun on her face. Could she do anything to change his mind?

She curled her fingers into her palms and looked out at the Christmas lights along Rice Street. Once Eva was safely home, she would do everything in her power to show him she loved him. If she had it to do over again, she would do it all differently. He'd been right about the police. They needed Ron to find Eva. He'd been right about everything.

In the dark, taillights disappeared around the corner ahead of them. She leaned forward. "Is that them?"

Ron accelerated. "I think so."

She gripped Bane's hand as the car zoomed ahead. Residents lined the streets, waiting for the Christmas parade to start, and several shouted and shook their fists at them. The speed limit was only twenty through here, and no one on the island drove more than forty-five anywhere, not even the highways.

They followed him out of town, then the lights turned into Smith's Luau. She pointed. "There's the car, but why would he go there?"

Bane leaned forward. "The garden is large, and there will be a lot of people. Maybe he thinks he can lose us."

"Not with Eva. She'll scream the minute she gets out of the car."

But the car ahead of them drove past the luau. Bane pointed. "He's going to the river."

Leia caught a glimpse of her sister's blond hair in the security light before she was hustled from sight and pushed into the bottom of a boat. "Hurry! He's getting away."

"I'm going as fast as I can," Ron said. "The accelerator is on the floorboard."

The tires skidded as they reached the parking lot, and Ron pulled the car to a stop under a light. The smell of burning rubber wafted up her nose as she threw open the door and clambered out on her side. "Eva!" A faint scream came to her ears. "We're coming, Eva!"

Leia's lungs constricted as she ran to the canoes. The other boat had disappeared in the darkness. Bane was beside her untying the canoe and grabbing an oar.

"I've called for backup," Ron yelled. He grabbed her arm and helped her into the canoe, then followed her.

The canoe rocked and she grabbed at the side. "Hurry, Bane!"

He tossed the rope into the canoe and stepped onto

the bottom of the boat. She leaned over so he could get to the back of the boat. "I'll steer, you paddle."

Bane's muscular arms flexed as he bent into the rowing. She moved the paddle and guided them to the center of the Wailua River. She'd never been on the river at night, and it was disorienting not to see the bank very well. The gnarled trees seemed to be reaching for them as if to stop them from catching up with Fletcher and Chambers.

Her muscles tightened at what sounded like a scream ahead. "What if he's drowning her?"

Bane redoubled his efforts at the oar. There was a splash ahead. Leia stood and strained her eyes trying to see. "Eva!"

The hair stood on end on her neck at the blood-curdling scream that slashed the silence. "Eva!"

Her sister couldn't be more than twenty feet ahead, but it was a dark, cloudy night and Leia could barely see her hand in front of her face.

"Leia, sit down! You're going to tip us." Bane's voice was hoarse.

She ignored his order and kicked off her slippers. "I'm going in! Ron, you take the stern."

"Leia, no! We're nearly there."

"He's killing her!" she screamed when her sister cried out again.

Without wasting another moment, she dove into the river. The warm water closed over her head, and she kicked to the surface, then struck out with strong strokes. Splashing sounded ahead to her right, and she veered that direction, shouting her sister's name. The other canoe loomed out of the darkness, just five feet away. She saw no figures in the boat, so they all must be in the water.

She treaded water and tried to get her bearings by sound alone. Frantic splashing came from the other side of the canoe. She submerged to swim without noise to the other side. Her head broke the surface, and she saw movement to her right. Then an oar came out of nowhere and struck her head.

The pain made her gasp, and her vision began to dim. Her muscles slackened, but before her eyes closed, Fletcher's grinning face mocked her.

~*~

"Hardheaded, stubborn woman," Bane muttered, throwing the oar to the bottom of the canoe.

"She's got guts." Ron's voice came out of the darkness, and a shadow moved as he shifted. "You picked a good one there."

Bane kicked off his slippers and slipped into the

water. The least amount of noise he could make, the better. The water was a silken caress around his limbs as he did a noiseless breaststroke toward where Leia had disappeared.

"Let go of my sister!" Eva yelled.

Her voice was to his right, but Bane circled around the other way. He had a sixth sense of another presence in that direction. Fletcher or Chambers? He kicked his legs and propelled himself through the calm water. A rooster crowed from the bank to his left. The sound oriented him to the distance to the shore. About fifteen feet. Could they be taking Eva and Leia to the other bank?

He paused and tried to see. Something moved about five feet away. After inhaling a deep breath, he dove deep and kicked toward the sound. His outstretched hand touched a thick ankle. His fingers closed around it, and he pulled down with all his might and dove hard for the bottom.

The man kicked to try to break Bane's grip, but Bane gritted his teeth and hung on. He was an expert free diver and had better lung capacity than this out-of-shape ex-con. He held the man to the bottom until he quit struggling and air began to bubble from the guy's mouth, then Bane shot to the top with the limp figure and swam to the shore. He staggered to the shore and threw the man to the mud.

When he started to turn to dive back to find Leia, the moon came from behind a cloud. The dim glow touched the face of a figure lying along the bank. "Leia!"

In two steps he was by her side. He knelt next to her and touched her face. It was still warm, and her chest rose and fell with her breaths. "Thank God you're alive."

"Such a touching reunion," a sneering male voice said behind him.

He whirled and saw the barrel of a gun aimed at his chest. Behind it was Fletcher's gloating face. "The police know about you, Fletcher. And so does your parole officer."

The man shrugged. "So what? I'll be dead in three months. Thanks to you two, I got hepatitis in prison. Destroyed my liver."

"It's not our fault you went to jail. You chose to break the law."

Fletcher bared his teeth. "You think you're so much better than everybody. But look who's in control now!" He gestured with the gun. "Roll Chambers over. I want to see if you killed him."

"He's not dead." Bane stepped over to where the inert man lay and prodded him with a bare foot, then rolled him over. Chambers moaned, but his eyes stayed closed. "See?"

"I'm through with him anyway." Fletcher turned the

gun on his partner's head, and a muffled shot rang out. "You're next, but first we're going to have a little fun."

Bane's ears rang. "What did you do to Leia? And where's Eva?"

"You'll see soon enough. Grab your girlfriend and come with me."

Backup was coming. Ron would be along with more police any minute. But would he look this way, or would they search the water first? Bane had to keep them all alive until he could get the gun or get help. He moved to Leia's side and sat her up.

Her head rolled to the side but her eyes fluttered open. There was no recognition in her eyes at first, then her lids flew open. "Bane! Where's Eva?" Her voice was groggy.

"We're about to find out. Can you stand?"

"I-I think so."

He helped her to her feet and supported her as they moved along the path between two giant trees. "Where are we going?"

"Shut up and walk." Fletcher prodded Bane's back with the gun.

Bane glanced around for something to use as a weapon. He'd never be able to grab a branch before Fletcher put a bullet in him. A man with nothing to lose was the most dangerous of all. No wonder Fletcher hadn't cared about breaking his parole.

They reached a clearing in the trees, and a small building crouched at the back. Back in the nineties, Hurricane 'Iniki had blown off most of the roof and the windows and the door, but it still stood. A light shone out of the broken glass of the windows. He saw a blond woman tied up and quickened his pace, urging Leia faster. She would want to make sure Eva was all right.

They stumbled through the shack's doorway. Chicken feathers and debris littered the interior. Eva sat bound to a chair at a table that leaned drunkenly to one side, two legs off.

Eva lifted her head at the noise, and her eyes widened. "Leia!"

Leia leaped forward and reached her sister. She knelt beside her. "You're alive." Her fingers tore at the ropes, but she made little headway on the tight knots.

Bane turned to face his captor. He had to find a way to disarm him. He sidled toward a table leg lying on the floor. "Why bring us here? Why not drown us?"

"I have something more fun in mind. Like letting Leia here watch her sister die. Then you can watch me shoot Leia. I'll save you for last, then wait for the police. I'm sure they're on their way."

Moe aimed the gun at Eva as Bane lunged for the table leg.

NINE

LEIA STEPPED IN FRONT OF HER SISTER WITH HER ARMS outstretched. She stared in horror as Fletcher took a step toward them. His finger moved on the trigger.

Bane seemed to sag forward as if he'd been hurt, then grabbed the chair leg by his feet. In one motion, he snatched up the chair leg and brought it around in an arc aimed at Fletcher's wrist. The wooden leg struck Fletcher's hand, but he managed to hang on to the gun. Bane leaped onto him, and the two struggled over the weapon.

Leia turned back to her sister and tore into the ropes with new fury. The thick fiber cut into her fingertips but finally began to loosen. She unraveled one knot. There was grunting and cursing on the floor behind her as Fletcher fought to retain possession of the gun. Bane was bigger and stronger, though, so she could only pray he would prevail. The last knot gave way, and she yanked the bonds away from Eva's wrist, then lifted her sister to her feet.

She cupped Eva's face in her hands. "Let's get outside. Hurry."

Eva nodded and threw her arms around Leia. "You came."

"I told you I would." Leia quickly disentangled from Eva's embrace and supported her as they turned for the door. They had to get help.

Locked in struggle, Bane and Fletcher rolled toward her, and she pressed Eva forward even faster. Then they were through the doorway. The night air touched her face, but there was no sign of any police yet. She shoved Eva into the yard. "Scream as loud as you can! We have to get the police here."

She rushed back to help Bane. The only weapon she could see was the chair, so she picked it up and held it over her head, waiting for the right moment to use it. Outside, Eva was shrieking at the top of her lungs. Her scream was loud enough to call anyone within ten miles.

Bane landed a punch on Fletcher's face, then rolled on top of him and pinned his arms down. "Give it up, Fletcher," he panted. He'd lost the gun somewhere.

"Never!" Fletcher managed to get one hand loose, and he jabbed Bane in the chin.

Bane fell off, and Fletcher scrambled to his feet. He grabbed another broken piece of chair leg from the floor and waved it menacingly in Bane's direction. Neither man had possession of the gun, and Leia looked around for it. It had to be here somewhere. She finally spied it under the table, so she dove onto her stomach for it just as Fletcher made a swipe at Bane with the poker.

Bane feinted left, then his big hand grabbed the poker and yanked it out of Fletcher's grip. He tossed it aside and leaped at the other man again. Leia's fingers closed around the gun, and she backed out from under the table. The grit and debris on the floor bit into her knees.

She sat up breathlessly, then got to her feet with the gun pointed toward the struggling men. She didn't know how to use it, but it looked menacing. If only she could get it to Bane, but the two men were locked in mortal combat. Fletcher wouldn't give up unless he was unconscious or dead.

She hovered five feet away from the struggling men. The discarded chair leg was at her feet, so she picked that up too and stood waiting for her chance to help.

Bane grunted as Fletcher rolled on top of him.

Fletcher lifted Bane's head and slammed it against the floor. Bane's gaze locked with Leia's. *Shoot*, he mouthed.

Leia looked at the gun in her hand. What if she hit Bane? She wasn't that good of a shot. Fletcher smacked Bane's head down against the floor again. Bane flung out a hand as if stunned, but Leia caught his eye again. In an instant, she dropped the gun into his hand.

He brought it up and aimed it at Fletcher. "Back against the wall."

The glee faded from Fletcher's face. He held his hands up and got to his feet.

Bane stood with his chest heaving. "Hand me that rope, would you?"

Leia dropped the poker and grabbed the rope. When she handed it to him, he grinned. "Annie Oakley, you're not."

"I have never held a gun before. I don't like it much."

"Glad we didn't have to use it." He tied up Fletcher and stepped back. "Eva okay?" Bane tipped his head to one side. "I can hear her screeching. Nothing wrong with those lungs at least. The police should be here any minute. They had to have heard her from the lake."

She heard some shouts. "I think that's them now." The fight seemed to have gone on forever, but she knew it couldn't have been longer than five minutes at the most. "Thank you for saving her, Bane. You were right. I needed you. I needed the police." She hesitated a moment. "I need to get to Eva."

She hurried away before he could answer.

ℐℓℓ

An ambulance with flashing lights was outside the shack. Bane tried to stay out of the way under the spreading branches of an *'ohi'a* tree as police tromped back and forth gathering evidence, though they had plenty of witnesses that Fletcher shot Chambers. Kaia had picked up Leia and Eva and taken them back to the house so she could fuss over them. Mano stayed behind to ride home with Bane.

Bane couldn't forget the expression on Leia's face before she left. He wished they could go back to the way things were last week.

Mano's expression was grim when he joined Bane under the tree. "Pretty cold to shoot him in the head when he was unconscious."

"Chambers was going to kill us too. Fletcher says he's dying. The police say that's true. He had a run-in with another guy at the prison. The guy arranged for him to get stuck with a dirty needle, and he got a virulent form of hepatitis that ravaged his liver. He probably won't be alive in three months."

Bane watched as two police officers marched Fletcher off with his hands cuffed behind his back. They put him in a police car. He stared balefully back at Bane as the car pulled away down the dirt track.

"Scary guy," Mano commented. "You look a little beat up."

Bane touched his swelling eye. "Could have been worse."

"Yeah." Mano's perusal grew intense. "I don't like to pry, but are things okay between you and Leia? You both seemed a little tense."

"The wedding is off," Bane blurted out.

Mano went quiet. He scuffed his flip-flop in the dirt a moment, then shook his head. "Doesn't seem right, brah. I've never seen you happier than you've been with her. You want to talk about it?"

"What's to talk about? She shut me out of her life deliberately."

"Women process things differently than we do."

"Spoken by a man with a whole two years of marriage under his belt." Bane grinned to deflect any sting in his words, then his smile faded and he shook his head. "She lied to me, Mano. Let me believe—let all of us believe—Eva had likely drowned from jumping off the Point. She was willing to call off the wedding rather than trust me with the truth. That's hard to get past."

"This is about Mom, isn't it?"

Bane shrugged and grabbed his brother's forearm. "Let's get out of the way. We'll go down by the river."

Tree frogs set up a cacophony as they walked down to the river. The moon glimmered on the water, and fish splashed off to their left.

Bane and Mano settled on rocks along the water's edge. At least he wouldn't be overheard here. He didn't feel good talking about Leia where someone might hear. It was too personal.

He picked up a flat stone and sent it skipping across the water. "Do you trust Annie to never leave you?"

Mano inhaled sharply. "Well, sure. I wouldn't have married her if I didn't believe that."

"I'm not so sure about Leia. I thought I knew her. That I would be the first person she turned to in trouble, just like she is the first one I would turn to. Then I found out she lied. Again."

"What do you mean again?"

"I dated her once before. She didn't want to get too close because she intended to never marry and have kids. The genetic defects in her family. So Leia chose the easy way out and never talked to me about it. What kind of marriage would we have if she's afraid to talk to me about what matters?"

Bane's chest felt heavy. Life had been so full of hope

and joy just last week. How could it have disintegrated into this morass of unhappiness so quickly?

"I kind of understand what happened, though, can't you? The guy convinced her Eva would die if she didn't do as she was told. She came from a traditional Hawaiian family. She's used to obeying authority. What would you have done if someone took Kaia and told you if you didn't follow his instructions, he'd kill her?"

Bane started to answer glibly, then paused to really consider the question. What would he do if his beloved sister were in the hands of some kind of maniac? Especially if she were handi-capped and frightened like Eva? He'd want to get her back as quickly as possible. If the kidnapper had said no police, would he have called the police immediately?

He shook his head. "I guess I wouldn't have told the police. But I would have told Leia."

"Even if you were told not to?"

"Even then. Together we would hatch a plan to make it appear we were following the guy's instructions, but we would have searched high and low for her."

"But you're, well, you. A big, capable guy with resources to track your sister down by yourself. Leia thought her best chance of getting her sister back was doing exactly what the kidnapper said. We know now he always planned to kill you both and intended to cause as much pain along the way as he could. If you let him break up you and Leia, he'll have won."

Bane picked up another rock and felt its smooth, round edges for a moment before he sent it skipping across the water. It skipped four times, then sank. Right now he felt like that stone—jittering over an unknown surface and headed for who knew where. But Leia was his compass and with her, he knew where he was headed.

He turned and looked at his brother. "I love her, you know."

"Of course you do. Otherwise this wouldn't have hurt so much. You can get past this, Bane. There are little hurts in any relationship, but you talk about it and work through them." Mano stood and extended his hand.

Bane took his brother's hand and got to his feet. "You're a good brother, brah."

"I know." Mano pointed at Bane's swelling eye. "Good thing I have the brains *and* the brawn in this family."

TEN

THE GUEST ROOM WINDOW WAS OPEN, AND THE SWEET scent of plumeria wafted in soothingly. Christmas lights festooned the palm tree outside the window and cast a comforting glow into the bedroom.

Leia tucked the clean white sheet around her sister, then smoothed the white-blond hair away from Eva's face. She leaned over to kiss her forehead. "Rest now, sweetheart. You're safe."

Eva's guileless blue eyes held worry as she stared up into Leia's face. "Are you sad, Leia? You look sad."

Leia forced a smile. "I'm very happy you're home safe and sound. It was a scary thing for you to have to go through. But we're all okay now."

Eva nodded. "And the wedding will be soon. We have lots and lots to do. I need to try on my dress again."

She'd tried it on at least twenty times. The cornflower blue bridesmaid dress had lace flounces, and Eva loved to twirl in it like a princess.

Leia's smile faded. How did she tell Eva there would be no wedding? She wouldn't understand. Tears prickled along the backs of Leia's eyes. "Um, about the wedding . . ."

A tap sounded on the door, and she turned to see Bane standing in the open doorway. Joy surged through her at the sight of his broad shoulders and thick shock of black hair. He needed a shave, but she'd never seen him look handsomer.

Now that she'd lost him.

Eva sat up and held out her arms. "Bane!"

He crossed the room in five strides and sat on the edge of the bed, then embraced her. "Hey, squirt. You don't look any the worse for wear."

"I am, though. Look." Eva showed him her arm where lurid bruises shaped like fingers marred the pale skin.

His mouth flattened and his eyes narrowed. He shot a glance at Leia. "That'll heal up just fine."

Eva's fingers touched the bruise around his eye. "Fletcher hit you. He's a bad, bad man."

"The police will make sure he never hurts you again."

Leia studied him as he soothed her sister and kissed

her good night. He seemed different somehow tonight. More relaxed without that harsh line to his mouth she'd seen for the past three days. She hovered near the bed until he gave Eva a final kiss, then rose and moved toward the door.

She followed him. "Good night, sweetheart."

"Night, Leia. Night, Bane." Her eyes closed, and Eva rolled to her side. "I didn't miss the wedding. Or Christmas."

Leia smiled and pulled the door shut as they exited the room. "I can't believe this is over." She glanced up at him. "Well, almost over. We still have some wedding plans to cancel. I need to call my parents and tell them not to fly over. And you—" She cut off what she was about to say when Bane put his fingers on her lips.

"I want to talk to you. Come with me." He led her through the living room and outside to the steps that went down to the ocean.

The sound of the sea rose in a crescendo with the storm surge still kicking up the waves. Whitecaps gleamed in the moonlight. It was a night very much like this one when Bane had proposed to her. He was still holding her hand. Did that mean anything, or was he merely being solicitous about her safety on the uneven ground?

They reached the *imu* pit area where his grandfather

and his father's father before him had cooked the luau pig for generations. Someone had already lit a fire, though she saw no one around. Even his grandfather's house was dark and quiet. The old man had gone to bed long ago.

"Have a seat."

She settled on a log and looked out over the water. Hope was nearly impossible to kill in the spirit, though she tried to keep hold of the way hers wanted to rise in her chest.

He sat on the log next to her and reached behind him, pulling up his 'ukulele. His fingers strummed the strings for a few moments. She kept her gaze on the strong lines and planes of his face. He was so dear and so handsome. His strong legs stretched out past his shorts, and his feet were bare.

She swallowed hard. "Did you do all this? Light the fire and lay out the seating?"

He nodded, his dark eyes on her. "Mano talked some sense into me tonight. We're never going to see eye to eye about everything, babe. I'm going to do things that hurt you too—things you don't understand. But that doesn't mean I don't love you."

"I'm sorry I hurt you," she whispered. "I was operating on pure panic. I won't ever do that again, Bane, I promise."

"Even if you do, I'm going to love you through it." His gaze held hers. "I was wrong to push you away."

Tears welled in her eyes and blurred his face. He strummed the 'ukulele again and began to sing the song he'd written just for her, the one he'd sung the night he proposed. The Hawaiian song spoke of his great love and longing for her and ended with a proposal of marriage.

He laid the 'ukulele down on the sand. "Want to marry me after all?" His grin was teasing.

She leaped from the log and launched herself at him. They both fell onto the sand. His lips were salty with the sea when he kissed her. The heat between them was hotter than the sun at noonday, but she gave herself up to the passion in his kiss.

He pulled away first and gave a shaky laugh. "How much longer until that honeymoon?"

"Soon," she promised, and pulled his head back down for another kiss.

Leia peeked out the window of the suite at the Hyatt. The big rollers flowing onto the beach were a perfect backdrop to the white tents festooned with red poinsettia wreaths. Twinkling lights added another Christmas touch. Leia had ducked inside the tents earlier and gawked at the tables decorated in red and gold for Christmas.

"I keep pinching myself." She turned to smile at Eva. "I can't believe this is really happening."

Her sister preened in her lacy blue dress. "Your hair is really pretty, Leia."

Leia glanced in the mirror. Eva had curled it all over, then Leia pulled it back from her face so it cascaded down her back. They'd pinned white pikake blossoms among the strands. "I love it too. I couldn't have done it without you."

"Can I get your dress now?" When Leia nodded, Eva moved to the closet and pulled out the gown.

Leia had made it herself. It was *kapa*, the traditional Hawaiian cloth made from mulberry bark. She'd worked on it for months, making sure the color was a soft white and the material was as supple as buckskin. She'd infused the fabric with pikake as well, and the sweet fragrance filled the room. The supple cloth was as white as she could make it with multiple bleachings in the sun, and she'd painted a blue plumeria along one hip. The color matched Eva's dress. The effect was unique and striking. At least she thought so. No one had seen it except for Eva.

Her sister helped her get the dress on without

messing up her hair. She fastened the zipper in the back for Leia. When Leia spun around, Eva's eyes widened. "You are like the sun."

Leia's eyes filled with tears. "Thank you."

When the knock came on her door, she opened it and took her father's hand. "I'm ready."

His face beamed with pride as he looked her over. "I've never seen you more beautiful, honey. And this dress! I can't believe you made this by yourself. Your grandmother will be so proud. She's having a good day today too. I think she'll remember it."

The day couldn't have been more perfect. She took her father's right arm, and Eva took the left. "Let's get you married," he said.

People in the lobby of the hotel stopped and stared at her unique gown as she passed. Several took pictures, and she walked with her head erect, happy with her appearance for the first time in her life. Once they reached the beach, she took off her shoes and walked barefoot toward the arbor of poinsettias, greenery, and twinkling lights where her future waited. Friends and family lined both sides of the white runner that led to the minister. She smiled at her mother and sister.

One of Bane's friends played Wagner's "Bridal Chorus" on a 'ukulele. The crowd burst into applause and pointed out to sea. Leia turned to see an outrigger canoe closing rapidly on the wedding party. Two dolphins pulled it, and Mano was at the bow. He blew the traditional pu shell horn, then blew it again. The regal sound brought tears to her eyes.

Mano hopped overboard and swam to shore with the horn aloft, then, dripping wet, he stepped to his brother's side and winked at her.

Then she was there in front of Bane. His eyes were wide as he looked her up and down. "Oh, babe," he whispered. "I'm speechless."

She smiled at the love in his eyes. She saw no one else in that moment. It was only Bane's warm brown eyes staring into her soul.

The minister cleared his throat. "In Hawai'i the lei is given as a sign of eternal aloha, a symbol of how you weave your lives together forever."

Bane took the elaborate pikake lei from Mano and placed it around her neck. Her fingers closed around the ti leaf lei in Kaia's hand, and she slipped it over Bane's head.

"As you weave your lives together, may you always trust one another and be united as you journey toward the eternity God has promised." The pastor glanced at her father. "Who gives this woman to be married to this man?"

Her father squeezed her hand, then looked at the

minister. "Her mother and I do. And God himself." He transferred her hand to Bane's arm. "Take good care of her, son. She's most precious to me."

Bane's warm fingers closed over her hand. "And to me."

Together they stepped under the arbor. The ceremony passed in a blur as Leia looked into Bane's eyes and repeated the traditional vows. She wanted to remember these words and this moment forever, but she was mostly conscious of the press of his hand and the love in his eyes. The pastor spoke of the holiness of this night, and it seemed somehow even more fitting that their wedding was on Christmas Eve.

"Now I give you the traditional Hawaiian blessing," the minister said. "*E Ho'omau Maua Ke Aloha.* That means 'From this day, this night, forevermore together.' You may kiss the bride."

"Under the mistletoe?" Bane asked, sweeping her into his arms.

She hadn't realized there was mistletoe here, but she saw it as she tipped up her face to meet his. His lips came down on hers, softly at first, then with rising passion that spread heat through her chest, down her arms, and into her belly. The sensation was so intense she had to cling to him to keep from falling. When he lifted his head, she was breathless.

"I think I'd like you to do that again," she whispered.

His lips twitched. "I think you just gave me permission to kiss you like that all the time."

The 'ukulele sprang to life again as they turned to walk through the crowd of friends and family. Her face hurt from smiling so much as they accepted congratulations through the evening and mingled at the food tables. The party would run all night, but she suddenly wanted Bane all to herself. She led him off to a quiet corner.

"Is everything all right?"

Suddenly shy, she glanced down at her bare feet peeking out from under the hem of the dress. "Think you're strong enough to carry me to our room?"

"I think I can manage that." The glint in his eyes went from warm to lava hot. He swept her up and carried her toward the hotel amid the hoots and cheers of their guests.

Leia hid her face in his shoulder and gave one final wave to Eva. He carried her to the elevator amid the grins of the employees and guests of the hotel. They were the only ones in the elevator as it moved briskly to the sixth floor.

"Tired yet?" She brushed her lips across his.

"Not even close." The ardor in his gaze intensified as the elevator doors opened.

Their suite was two doors down. She fumbled the

key out of his pocket and unlocked it from her perch in his arms. He pushed into the suite and the door shut behind them.

This night would cement their love into a holy bond that would never be broken. Leia closed her eyes and clung to the promise of forever in his kiss.

Hawaiian Language
Pronunciation Guide

Although Hawaiian words may look challenging to pronounce, they're typically easy to say when sounded out by each syllable. The Hawaiian language utilizes five vowels (a, e, i, o, u) and seven consonants (h, k, l, m, n, p, w). Please note that sometimes the w is pronounced the same as v, as in Hawai'i.

a - ah, as in car: *aloha*
e - a, as in may: *nene*
i - ee, as in bee: *honi*
o - oh, as in so: *mahalo*
u - oo, as in spoon: *kapu*

Dipthongs: Generally, vowels are pronounced separately except when they appear together:

ai, ae - sounds like I or *eye*

ao - sounds like *ow* in *how*, but without a nasal twang

au - sounds like the *ou* in *house* or *out*, but without a nasal twang

ei - sounds like *ei* in *chow mein* or in *eight*

eu - has no equivalent in English, but sounds like *eh-oo* run together as a single syllable

iu - sounds like the *ew* in *few*

oi - sounds like the *oi* in *voice*

ou - sounds like the *ow* in *bowl*

ui - an unusual sound for speakers of English, sort of like the *ooey* in *gooey*, but pronounced as a single syllable.

CHARACTERS:

Anaki (ah-NAH-kee)

Bane (BAH-AH-nay)

Kaia (KIGH-yah)

Liko (LEE-ko)

Mahina (MAH-HEE-nah)

Mano (m-AH-no)

Nahele (nah-HAY-lay)

Oke (OH-kay)

Paie (PIE-ay)

Words used in this series:

aloha (ah-LOW-hah): a warm Hawaiian greeting or parting; love, grace, sentiment, compassion, sympathy, kindness, affection, friendship; to show kindness or to remember with affection.

aloha nô (ah-LOW-ha-NO): expression of sympathy

auê (au-(W)EH): uh-oh, or oops

brah (bra): brother

haole (ha-OH-lay): white person. Can be a slur depending on tone.

he aha ke 'no (HAY-ah-ha-KAY-ah-no): What is the kind? Meaning, what kind of nonsense is this?

ho'oponopono (HO-oh-PO-no-PO-no): ritual of family therapy. Literally means "to make things right."

imu pit (EE-moo): pit for roasting a pig at a lu'au

keiki (KAY-kee): child

keikikane (KAY-kee-KAH-nay): son

lei aloha (lay ah-LOW-hah) beloved child

mahalo (mah-HAH-low): thank you. Heard everywhere in the islands, even when something is announced on the loud speaker in Kmart.

makuahine (mah-koo-ah-HEE-nay): mother

makuahini (ma-koo-ah-HEE-nee): mother

makuakane (mah-koo-ah-KAH-nay): father

'ono (OH-no): a popular fish for eating

tûtû (too-too): grandma.

tûtû kâne (too-too-KAH-nay): grandpa

READING GROUP GUIDE

1. Was Leia right to try to obey the kidnapper? Why or why not?
2. What is the difference between forgiving and forgetting after someone hurts you? Is it possible to forget?
3. Bane felt marriage had to be based on trust. Why is that important in a marriage?
4. Do we ever get over childhood hurts?
5. What do you think are the biggest differences between men and women?

ACKNOWLEDGMENTS

I HAVE TO ESPECIALLY THANK MICHELLE LIM FOR HER great brainstorming assistance when I began thinking about this novella. I was in Duluth teaching at an author's retreat when I heard the news that I got to write another story in Rock Harbor. Michelle had read all the Rock Harbor novels and helped me come up with the plot. Thanks so much, Michelle! You rock!

And thanks to my great team at Thomas Nelson who love Rock Harbor as much as I do. Thanks for being so quick to jump in and get this story ready. It was so fun to get to go back to that special place. Thanks, Ami and Daisy!

And a special thanks to editor Julee Schwarzburg

who agreed to step in quickly to edit the manuscript. I don't know what I would have done without you!

For my readers who never tire of Bree and the gang in Rock Harbor.

Thank you for your devotion!

THE ALOHA REEF SERIES

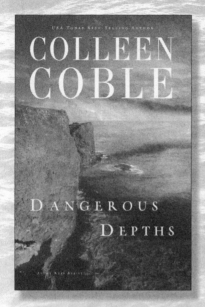

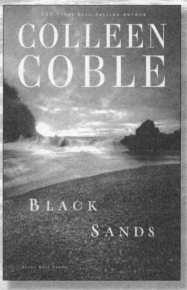

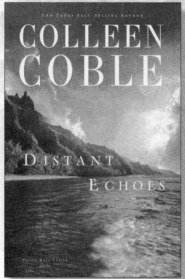

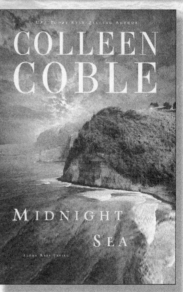

AVAILABLE IN PRINT AND E-BOOK

THOMAS NELSON
Since 1798

The *USA Today* Bestselling Hope Beach Series

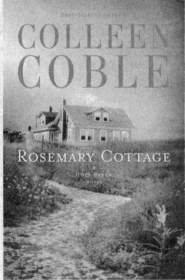

"**Atmospheric and suspenseful**"

—*Library Journal*

Available July 2014

Available in print and e-book

All is Calm

A Lonestar Christmas Novella

This Christmas, Lauren seeks sanctuary and finds
unexpected romance at the Bluebird Ranch.

Coming November 2014
Available in E-Book Only

THOMAS NELSON
Since 1798

A vacation to Sunset Cove was her way of celebrating and thanking her parents. After all, Claire Dellamore's childhood was like a fairytale. But with the help of Luke Elwell, Claire discovers that fairytale was really an elaborate lie . . .

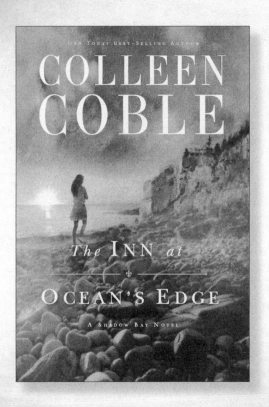

The first Sunset Cove Novel

Available April 2015

Thomas Nelson
Since 1798

ONE

The constriction around her neck tightened, and she tried to get her fingers under it to snatch a breath. She was losing consciousness. A large wave came over the bow of the boat, and the sea spray struck her in the face, reviving her struggle. She had to fight or he would kill her. She could smell his cologne, something spicy and strong. His ring flashed in the moonlight, and she dug the fingers of her right hand into his red sweater. The pressure on her neck was unrelenting. She was going to die.

ELIN SUMMERALL BOLTED UPRIGHT IN THE BED. HER heart pounded, and she touched her throat and found it smooth and unharmed. It was just that dream again. She was safe, right here in her own house on the outskirts of Virginia Beach, Virginia. Her slick skin glistened in the moonlight streaming through the window.

The incision over her breastbone pulsed with pain,

and she grabbed some pills from the bedside and swallowed them. *In and out.* Concentrating on breathing helped ease both her pain and her panic. She pulled in a breath, sweetly laden with the scent of roses blooming outside her window, then lay back against the pillow.

Her eyes drifted shut, then opened when she heard the tinkle of broken glass. Was it still the dream? Then the cool rush of air from the open window struck her face, and she heard a foot crunch on broken glass.

She leaped from the bed and threw open her door. Her heart pounded in her throat. Was an intruder in the house? In her bare feet, she sidled down the hall toward the sound she'd heard. She paused to peek in on her four-year-old daughter. One arm grasping a stuffed bear, Josie lay in a tangle of princess blankets.

Elin relaxed a bit. Maybe she hadn't heard glass break. It might still have been part of the nightmare. She peered around the hall corner toward the kitchen. A faint light glimmered as if the refrigerator stood open. A cool breeze wafted from the kitchen, and she detected the scent of dew. She was sure she'd shut and locked the window. The hair stood on the back of her neck, and she backed away.

Then a familiar voice called out. "Elin? I need you."

Relief left her limp. Elin rushed down the hall to the kitchen where her mother stood in front of the back door with broken glass all around her feet. The refrigerator stood open as well. Her mom's blue eyes were cloudy with confusion, and she wrung her hands as she looked at the drops of blood on the floor.

Elin grabbed a paper towel. "Don't move, Mom. You've cut yourself." She knelt and scooped the bits of glass away from her mother's bleeding feet. Her mother obediently sat in the chair Elin pulled toward her, and she inspected the small cuts. Nothing major, thank goodness. She put peroxide on her mother's cuts and ushered her back to bed, all the while praying that when morning came, her mother's bout with dementia would have passed. For now.

It was only when she went back to the hall that she smelled a man's cologne. She rushed to the kitchen and glanced around. The glass in the back door was shattered. *Inwardly.*

He's been in the house.

$\sim \!\! \mathcal{O} \mathcal{C} \!\! \sim$

The neat plantation-style cottage looked much the same as the last time Marc Everton had been here. Seeing Elin Summerall again hadn't even been on his radar when he pulled on his shoes this morning, but his investigation had pulled up her name, and he needed to find out what she knew.

He put the SUV in Park and shut off the engine. Blue flowers of some kind grew along the brick path to the front door. A white swing swayed in the breeze on the porch.

He mounted the steps and pressed the doorbell. He heard rapid footsteps come his way. The door swung open, and he was face-to-face with Elin again after all this time. She was just as beautiful as he remembered. Her red hair curled in ringlets down her back, and those amazing aqua eyes widened when she saw him.

She leaned against the doorjamb. "Marc, what a surprise." Her husky voice squeaked out as if she didn't have enough air. Her gaze darted behind her, then back to him. "W-What are you doing here?"

"I needed to talk to you. Can I come in?"

She swallowed hard and looked behind her again. "I'll come out." She slipped out the door and went to the swing, where she curled up with one leg under her, a familiar pose.

He perched on the porch railing. "I-I was sorry to hear about Tim. A heart attack, I heard. Strange for someone so young."

She nodded. "His lack of mobility caused all kinds of health problems." She glanced toward the house again and bit her lip.

The last time he'd seen her she was pregnant. And

Tim had thrown him off the premises. While Marc understood the jealousy, it had been a little extreme.

His jaw tightened. "I'll get right to the point. I'm investigating Laura Watson's murder. I saw a news story this morning about you receiving her heart."

She gulped and clutched her hands in her lap. "That's right. What do you mean 'investigating'?"

"I'm with the FBI."

"I thought . . ." She bit her lip and looked away. "I mean, you used to be in the Air Force."

"I was ready for something new."

"Sara never told me you'd left the military."

He lifted a brow but said nothing. He doubted he'd often been the topic of conversation between his cousin and Elin. Eyeing her, he decided to lay his cards on the table. "My best friend was murdered while investigating this case. My supervisor thinks I can't be objective now and wouldn't assign me to the case, but he's wrong. I took some leave, and I'm going to find his killer."

She gulped. "Oh, Marc, I'm so sorry."

He brushed off her condolences. "The article said you received Laura's heart, that you've been having some kind of memories of the murder."

Her face paled, but her gaze stayed fixed on him. "Yes, it's been a little scary."

"Sorry to hear you've been sick. You all right now?"

When she nodded, a long curl fell forward, spiraling down her long neck to rest near her waist. He yanked his gaze back from that perfect, shining lock. Her hair was unlike any other woman's he'd ever met. Thick and lustrous with a color somewhere between red and auburn and lit from within by gold highlights.

Her hand went to the center of her chest. "I had a virus that damaged my heart. I'm still recovering from surgery, but the doctors are pleased with my progress."

"That's good." He pushed away the stab of compassion. The only reason he was here was to find out what she knew about the murder. "So tell me about these visions or whatever they are."

~ 𝒥𝓁𝓁 ~

Elin exhaled and forced her tense shoulder muscles to relax. She had to do this. But what if she told him everything and he didn't believe her? No one else had listened. Was it because she didn't know herself anymore and it came across to others?

His dark good looks, only enhanced by a nose that had been broken several times, had always drawn female attention. She'd vowed they would never turn her head, but she was wrong. So wrong. He'd haunted her dreams for nearly five years, and she thought she'd finally put the guilt to rest. But one look at his face had brought it surging back. The scent of his cologne, Polo Red, wafted to her, instantly taking her back to that one night of passion.

She'd been so young and stupid. They hadn't even liked each other, and to this day, she wondered what had gotten into her.

Marc opened the iPad in his hand and launched a program. "How did you find out she was your donor?"

"I have access to the records, and no one thought to lock me out." She twisted her hands together. "To explain this, I need to give you some background, so bear with me." She plunged in before he could object. "I've worked matching up donors with recipients for five years. I love my job."

"I know."

Those two words told her a lot. "Anyone who works with organ donation has heard the stories. They've even hit the news on occasion. Accounts of things the recipient knew about the donor. Things they should have had no way of knowing."

He nodded. "Cell memory."

At least he knew the term. "That's right. Within hours of receiving my new heart, I started having flashbacks of Laura's murder." She touched her throat. "I'm choking, fighting for my life. I remember things like the color of the murderer's hair. I keep smelling a man's cologne. I went to the department store to identify it. It's Encounter." She saw doubt gathering on his face and hurried on. "He was wearing a sweater the night he killed her. It was red."

He lifted a brow. "A sweater? On a Caribbean cruise?"

She bit her lip. "Maybe he put it on to prevent being scratched. I fought—I mean, Laura fought—very hard."

He didn't believe her. He hadn't taken a single note on his iPad. She had to convince him or Josie would be orphaned. Mom would have to go to a nursing home. "He's stalking me."

His somber gaze didn't change. "What's happened?"

"Someone broke into my house the other night. I'd just had a nightmare about the murder, and I heard the glass break. At first I thought it was an intruder, then Mom called for me. I found her in the kitchen in the middle of broken glass. I cleaned her up and got her to bed before I looked around more." She shuddered and hugged herself. "The glass in the back door had been broken from outside. He'd been here."

"What makes you think it's the man who killed Laura?"

"Who else could it be? He knows I'm remembering things because it was in the newspaper. He has to silence me before I remember everything."

He closed the cover on his tablet. "Well, thank you for answering my questions, Elin. I'll look into your claims. I've heard about cell memory, but most doctors consider it part of the psychological trauma from organ transplants. Have you been to a doctor? Maybe the intruder the other night was a nightmare. You said you'd been dreaming. And he wasn't actually *in* the house, was he?"

She stayed put in the swing. "You have to believe me. I know I sound like I'm crazy, but it's all too real."

His mouth twisted. "The police didn't believe you either, did they?"

She shook her head. "But they don't know me. You do."

His eyes went distant. "I'm not sure I do either. You seem—different somehow."

Her eyes burned. Everyone said that, but she didn't *feel* any different. Okay, maybe some of her likes and dislikes had changed, but it meant nothing. She was still Elin Summerall, Josie's mommy and Ruby's daughter.

The front door opened, and she saw her daughter's small hand on the doorknob. *No, no, Josie, don't come out.* Her daughter emerged with a bright smile. The red top and white pants she wore enhanced her dark coloring. Her distinctive hazel eyes were exactly like the man's in front of her. Maybe he wouldn't notice. A futile hope. Marc was a good detective, the best. Tenacious too.

"Hi, honey. Mommy is busy. Go back inside with Grandma."

Josie's eyes clouded. "She's sleeping. I want to go to the park."

Marc's gaze swept over Josie and lingered on her widow's peak. "This is Josie?"

There was no escaping this reckoning. "Yes. Josie, say hello to Mr. Everton."

"Hi, Mr. Everton. You want to come to my birthday party? I'll be five next month."

His smile was indulgent. "What's the date?"

"July 10."

His eyes widened, and Elin could almost hear the wheels spinning in his head, see him calculating the time. Tim hadn't come back for a month after that night.

He bolted upright, and his hands curled into fists. "I'd love to, Josie." His voice was controlled, but the look he shot Elin was full of fury and disbelief.

Elin forced a smile. "Go inside, honey. We'll go to the park in a little while. I need to talk to Mr. Everton for a few minutes."

Her daughter gave a final pout, then turned and went back inside. The door banged behind her as a final punctuation of her displeasure.

The silence stretched between Elin and Marc as their gazes locked. How on earth did she begin?

He paced to the door and back, then dug into his pocket and popped a mint from its package. He popped it into his mouth. "She's my daughter and you never told me." He spat out the tight words, and a muscle in his jaw jumped.

~ollo~

Marc struggled to control his anger. He'd instantly recognized Josie's resemblance to him instead of her red-haired mother. And Tim had been blond. Josie's hazel eyes were flecked with green and gold, just like his. The dimple in her right cheek matched his. So did the shape of her face and her dark curls. And her widow's peak.

He paced the porch and looked at Elin. Her figure was enough to stop traffic, but their personalities had never really meshed. Except for that one night after her father died. Ravaged by grief, she'd shown up at his house looking for Sara, and he gave her a drink to calm her down. One drink led to another and another until they crossed a line of no return. A night they both regretted.

He saw hope and fear warring in her beautiful face. "Why?" His voice was hoarse, and he cleared his throat. "Why didn't you tell me?"

She bit her lip. "As far as I was concerned, Tim was

her father. That was one of the conditions he made before we were married, that he wanted her to be *his* daughter."

"He's been gone for two years. You could have come to me as soon as he died." His gaze swung back to the door. Elin had deprived him of two years he could have had with his daughter. His fists clenched again, and his throat ached from clenching his jaw.

Her eyes shimmered with moisture. "The last thing he asked me before he died was to never tell you. H-He was jealous. I'm sure you realized that when you came here with Sara that day and he went into a rage."

He gave a curt nod. "So you never planned to tell me?"

Her chin came up. "No. I'd betrayed Tim once. I didn't want to do it again."

The fact he had a child still floored him. What did he do with this? "I'll talk to my attorney and draw up some support papers."

A flush ran up her pale skin. "I don't want your money, Marc! Josie is *my* daughter. Tim is her daddy, and we don't need another one. The only thing I need from you is for you to find that man and put him behind bars before he hurts me."

"I intend to." Surely she wouldn't keep his daughter away from him? He wasn't going to be one of those deadbeat dads, no way. "But I'm not so sure about that cell-memory stuff."

She wrung her hands. "I see your skepticism. Don't you think I know it's crazy? Everyone just says, 'There, there, Elin. You've been through so much. This will pass.' But it's getting worse! The dreams come nearly every night. You have to help me."

Against his will, he saw the conviction in her face. So what if it was some kind of hallucination from the heart transplant? Josie was still his daughter. He owed it to her to see if there was any truth to this. And his lack of control that night still haunted him. Her grief for her father had been a poor excuse for what they'd done.

He went back to his perch on the porch railing and picked up his pen. "Start over from the beginning."

About the Author

RITA FINALIST COLLEEN COBLE IS THE AUTHOR OF several bestselling romantic suspense novels, including *Tidewater Inn*, and the Mercy Falls, Lonestar, and Rock Harbor series.